## Scandal at the Palace

*Royal romances fit for the headlines!*

Five years after the death of his wife, reclusive King Jozef is stepping out of the shadows back into the royal spotlight. For the sake of his grown-up sons, Axel and Liam, he'll show his citizens he's still alive and well, and even go on a date or two...

A secret fling with the PR woman sent to help him is *not* part of the plan...but is totally irresistible!

Read King Jozef and Rowan's story in
*His Majesty's Forbidden Fling*

And an unexpected and completely off-limits fling with his bodyguard leaves the playboy prince with all-too-real feelings...

Discover what happens in Axel and Heather's story

*Off-Limits to the Rebel Prince*

Available now!

Meanwhile, Prince Liam is embroiled in his own royal scandal.

Don't miss his story, coming soon!

Dear Reader,

After the wonderful story of Prince Axel Sokel's dad in *His Majesty's Forbidden Fling*, it was intimidating to begin looking for a story as strong for Axel. But once Heather walked onto the page—a bodyguard who'd served in a war and ruled the roost in a house with five brothers—I was as hooked as I knew Axel was going to be.

As a prince who was hounded by the press after his mother's death, Axel's jaded. But Heather's had such a difficult life that she doesn't merely see the wonder and majesty of Axel's world; she helps open his eyes to emotions and happiness stolen from him when his mom died.

How does she do it? And how does that result in a romance? Well, you'll have to read the book. But I will tell you this... It's when things go wrong that we show our true selves, and we can only find real love when we're ourselves.

Now I'll bet you're really curious! I hope you enjoy reading Axel's story as much as I did writing it!

*Susan*

# Off-Limits to the Rebel Prince

—

*Susan Meier*

Recycling programs
for this product may
not exist in your area.

ISBN-13: 978-1-335-73704-5

Off-Limits to the Rebel Prince

Copyright © 2023 by Linda Susan Meier

For questions and comments about the quality of this book, please contact us at CustomerService@Harlequin.com.

Harlequin Enterprises ULC
22 Adelaide St. West, 41st Floor
Toronto, Ontario M5H 4E3, Canada
www.Harlequin.com

Printed in U.S.A.

**Susan Meier** is the author of over fifty books for Harlequin. *The Tycoon's Secret Daughter* was a Romance Writers of America RITA® Award finalist, and *Nanny for the Millionaire's Twins* won the Book Buyers Best Award and was a finalist in the National Readers' Choice Awards. Susan is married and has three children. One of eleven children herself, she loves to write about the complexity of families and totally believes in the power of love.

### Books by Susan Meier

### Harlequin Romance

#### Scandal at the Palace

*His Majesty's Forbidden Fling*

#### A Billion-Dollar Family

*Tuscan Summer with the Billionaire*
*The Billionaire's Island Reunion*
*The Single Dad's Italian Invitation*

*Hired by the Unexpected Billionaire*
*Reunited Under the Mistletoe*
*One-Night Baby to Christmas Proposal*

Visit the Author Profile page
at Harlequin.com for more titles.

To my wonderful editor, Nicola Caws, who helps
me dig until I find the diamond in my rough ideas.

## Praise for
## Susan Meier

"The perfect choice. I read this in one sitting; once
I started, I couldn't put it down. *The Bodyguard
and the Heiress* will put a smile in your heart. What
I love most about Susan Meier's books is the
joy your heart feels as you take the journey with
characters that come to life. Love this book."

—*Goodreads*

# CHAPTER ONE

GIVING HIS WEEKLY Monday evening report as head of Castle Admin, Prince Axel Sokol sat on the chair across from his father, Jozef Sokol, the King of Prosperita, a thriving island country in the Mediterranean. Beside him sat his brother, Liam, a tall, thin blond with blue eyes, who would reign after their father resigned.

It might have appeared Axel was the proverbial spare child, born only to serve if something happened to Liam, but Axel had found his place and purpose three years ago when he'd taken over Castle Admin. That department managed every detail of royal life from organizing schedules and prepping for state dinners and embassy balls to providing security, particularly bodyguards.

There wasn't an aspect of his father or brother's lives he didn't know, but the safety of the current and future King was the number one priority of Castle Admin. That gave his job meaning. He'd lost his mother to cancer when he was a teenager. He wouldn't lose his dad. And he certainly wouldn't lose his brother.

He finished his report for the current summer season and his father sat forward. A tall man with dark hair and dark eyes, from whom Axel liked to think he'd gotten his good looks, King Jozef smiled. "Thank you, Axel. I've said it before, and I'll say it again. Our lives have never run more smoothly."

*Or been safer.* Axel could have added that. To him that was the most important job of running the castle. Making sure the well-known, well-liked King and the future King were guarded by the best. The world wasn't the simple place it had once been. Even as popular as King Jozef was, he still got the occasional death threat. There were still tourists who tried to climb the fences to get onto the castle grounds. Those might not be life-threatening, but they proved how determined people could be when they wanted something. Most intruders were harmless. But one day they could be terrorists, assassins or kidnappers. The tourists' attempts had shown Axel weaknesses in their compound and he and his staff were prepared.

"I think we need to shift the focus of this evening's meeting to a more pressing matter than the gardens."

Axel frowned. *That felt a little weird.* His father knew Castle Admin was more than housekeeping and gardening. He'd never so casually dismissed Axel's work before.

"Liam, you're over thirty now." The King sat back in his chair. "You haven't had a serious relationship in three years. Before you balk, it's your responsibility to produce an heir."

Axel coughed to hide a laugh. This was the benefit of not being his father's successor. He had a great job, a place in the administration and no one messed with his love life.

Liam said nothing. In the oppressive silence of his father's office, Axel slid a sideways glance over to his brother. The tips of his ears were red, meaning Liam was either embarrassed or furious. Neither was good.

Wanting to break the tension and help his brother, Axel joked, "Oh, he has plenty of time."

The King's eyebrows rose. "Not really. Ideally, the new heir will have years observing me, then his father, when Liam takes over. Even if Liam got married this year, he'd need nine months to produce a child…meaning when Liam's sixty, his child wouldn't even be thirty." He pointed at his watch. "You're on the clock."

Hearing the seriousness in his father's tone, Axel knew better than to keep up the jokes. He watched Liam swallow hard. The air in the room stilled and chilled.

His father sighed. "Liam, it's not like I'm asking for a detailed plan, but I don't feel you're taking this seriously."

Liam finally spoke. "I'm fine."

"Actually, that's my point," the King argued. "I don't think you are."

Angry, Liam bounced out of his seat. "What do you want from me? Names? A timetable? You and Rowan certainly didn't play by anybody's rules."

The chill in the room turned to ice. Axel worked to keep his mouth from falling open. Though he understood Liam's need to argue, mentioning their dad's clandestine romance with the current Queen was over the line.

Jozef said, "That's enough. What I want is to see you wake up and take responsibility." He pointed at Axel. "Look at your brother. He found a place. It might seem like only petty details to you and me, but he's at least doing something with his life."

Axel's breathing jerked to a stop. In three years, he'd always believed his father saw the importance of his position. But, of course, compared to Liam, Axel's job probably did appear to be petty details.

Still, the insult of it rattled through him.

Rising, the King said, "You're dismissed." He glanced at Axel. "Both of you."

Axel followed Liam out of their father's office. To look at them no one would guess they were brothers. Liam had short, neat yellow hair. Axel's thick black hair fell to his shoulders in a blunt cut. Liam's eyes were baby blue. Axel's were as dark as a moonless midnight. Both were tall, but Liam was thin. Axel liked his gym time.

And while Axel was always in motion, Liam was the calm one. A thinker who didn't make rash decisions or moves. But right now, Axel's brother virtually vibrated with anger.

Axel encouraged Liam up the hall, away from their father's office. "Sorry, Liam."

"It doesn't matter."

Axel winced. "Actually, I think it does. Dad doesn't bring things up lightly. He wants you to find a wife." He winced again before he jumped in with both feet. "Don't forget our parents' marriage was an arranged marriage."

Liam stopped and gaped at Axel. "You don't think he was hinting that if I didn't get serious with someone soon, he might force me into an arranged marriage?"

Axel motioned for Liam to start walking again. "I don't know what to think. But you've dated some of the most beautiful women in the world. I find it difficult to believe you can't fall in love."

"It's not hard to fall in love. It is hard to find a woman who wants this life."

With all the rules and restrictions the royals were honor-bound to follow, Axel had always suspected that might be true.

As they approached the ornate foyer with the

stairway leading to the private quarters of the royals, Axel stopped. Choosing his words carefully, he said, "I wouldn't want an arranged marriage, but if you think falling in love doesn't work to find a queen, maybe it would be easier to find someone willing to be a queen and go from there."

Liam's expression shifted with disappointment. "You think I need an arranged marriage?"

"I think Dad's right. You're over thirty now. It *is* time you settled down. If you don't want to go the arranged marriage route, at least start dating someone, instead of always playing the field."

Liam snorted. "Look who's talking. I don't think you've dated anyone more than a month in the past five years."

He grinned. "I haven't. But I also don't have to produce an heir."

"That's right," Liam scoffed. "You don't have to do anything."

That insult mixed and mingled with their dad's offhand comments about his job, his place, and hit Axel like a punch in the chest. The very people he was protecting didn't see the value of his work.

Liam stormed away and Axel took a quick breath. He could be running around Europe right now, dating supermodels. He could be gambling. He could be drinking every night and sleeping until noon, feeding the tabloids with a gossip-worthy life. Instead, he gave his time, his efforts, *his life* to protecting the two people who meant the most to him in the world.

Neither one even saw it, let alone appreciated it.

He used to be the rebel Prince. Now he was the dull Prince in charge of minutia no one cared about.

The temptation to resign rumbled through him. If they genuinely believed what he did wasn't important then why was he doing it? All these years, he'd thought he'd found his place in the royal family, found meaning and worthy purpose for his life.

But he hadn't. It seemed he'd given up everything for nothing.

Realizing he probably just needed a break, he ran up the stairs and back down the hall to his apartment. He shucked his black suit and put on a pair of shorts and an ugly button-down shirt with pineapples all over it. Then he tucked his hair up under an old fedora he'd sneaked out of his grandfather's closet.

Maybe he simply needed a few hours of being the rebel Prince?

For Heather Larson, there was nothing worse than guarding a client in a dark bar—unless she actually wasn't on duty or even in his detail. She'd followed Prosperita's second prince, Axel Sokol, when she caught him sneaking out of the palace, taking a cab to a car he had hidden, then driving to this hellhole.

But as a bodyguard for the royal family, she was incredibly glad she had. Poor lighting and shady characters were the tip of the iceberg in this place. The bartender's casual sleight of hand with his last customer could have concealed a drug handoff. The floor needed a good sweeping, which meant the tables were undoubtedly coated with spillage from last night's drinks—and God only knew what else.

Plus, there was a door—easy entry for anybody who knew about it or a quick exit if someone robbed the place. Probably at gunpoint from the appearances of the smattering of patrons.

The shifty-looking bartender poured Heather's beer and handed it to her. Grabbing some paper napkins, she turned and headed for a table in the corner. Prince Axel thought he was smarter than the team of bodyguards supplied by Castle Admin—probably because he was the *head* of Castle Admin. But apparently he could be as dumb as a rock. With his incredibly recognizable blunt cut shoulder-length black hair tucked under a scruffy fedora and his typical jeans and sweater replaced by cargo shorts and a tropical print shirt, he did look like a tourist. He'd obviously fooled the cabbie who'd picked him up a few blocks up the street from the castle. But there was something about the ease and sexuality in his walk that was a dead giveaway of his identity. Of course, the guys in this dingy bar weren't his typical fans. They wouldn't notice his walk, let alone identify it.

She took a seat at a table in the dark, dark corner, shaking her head as she drizzled hand sanitizer onto one of her napkins and swiped it over the top. Having never been on Axel's detail, she wasn't somebody the Prince knew. But just in case, she'd taken her long blond hair out of its professional "work" ponytail and let it hang to her belly button before she removed the jacket of the black suit worn by all the royal bodyguards along with the white shirt, leaving her in a pale blue tank top and black straight-leg pants.

After surveying the pool table, Axel leaned his cue stick against it, pulled back his arm and shoved the stick through his fingers. It struck the white ball, sending the other balls flying with a loud crack. A giggling waitress in short shorts set his beer on the rim of the pool table. Axel winked at her, casually taking the beer and setting it on a nearby table. He didn't criticize her poor choice of places to set a beer. He flirted.

Heather rolled her eyes. A gorgeous prince with the personality of a Casanova was the definition of trouble in a bar like this. The last thing she needed was a confrontation between her royal and a jealous boyfriend.

"Hey, baby."

She glanced up to see a good-looking guy with long curly blond hair and striking blue eyes grinning at her.

*Still? Hey, baby? Was it 1990 again?*

Not wanting to call attention to herself, she forced a smile. "Hey."

"Looking for company?"

She broadened the smile, hoping to take the sting out of her refusal. "No. Bad, bad day with my *boyfriend*." There. The mention of a boyfriend usually got rid of good-looking guys who believed every woman wanted them.

Not this one. Without being invited, he took a seat. "Maybe what you need is a real man."

She almost hurt herself stopping an eye roll. "What I need is twenty minutes to myself to enjoy my beer."

He reached over and took her hand.

Maybe if she sighed, he'd get the hint?

He didn't even notice. He ran his thumb over her palm. "Let's go someplace private where we can talk about this."

"No. Really. I'm fine."

"You sure are fine. Love the long hair. Love ladies with green eyes."

The time for subtlety was over. "And I'm not interested."

"Oh, sugar. Trust me, once we get started you will be."

"No."

As if she hadn't spoken, he rose and tried to yank her out of her seat.

He was stronger than he looked. Because she'd underestimated him, she just barely thwarted him. If he tried again, she'd have no choice but to jump into full-on bodyguard mode.

She attempted to defuse the situation one more time. "Come on. Seriously. I just want to drink my beer."

He yanked harder and hauled her out of her seat. "And I'm telling you I could give you the best time of your life—"

The sweet talker suddenly released her hand and flew backward. Heather leaped away from the table as her drink tipped over, and beer went everywhere. Her gaze jerked to her rescuer and of all the horrible things to see, Prince Axel was the one who'd tossed him across the room.

Damn it!

"Okay. I'm fine. No harm done," she said quickly, hoping to shift Axel's attention back to the pool game so she could leave and call her boss to send somebody else to the bar to guard the Prince.

"Are you sure?"

As his smooth voice drifted to her, beneath the rim of his fedora, his midnight-black eyes narrowed.

Double damn! If he kept staring at her, he'd

realize he knew her. He might not pinpoint why he knew her. She'd only been in the castle two months. But they'd crossed paths in the corridors a time or two.

Mr. Good-Looking found his footing and turned to rush Axel like a bull seeing a red flag.

Who was she kidding? Prince Axel recognizing her was the least of her worries.

She caught the Prince's arm, pulled him out of the way and all but threw him toward the door—which she really hoped was unlocked.

"Let's go."

Confused, he shook off her hand. "Go?"

She grabbed his arm again, this time in a death grip. He wouldn't escape this hold. "We need to get out of here."

They took a few steps, Mr. Good-Looking on their heels. Almost at the exit, she surveyed the customers again. Half appeared to be itching for a fight. The other half were already pressing toward them. Maybe friends of Mr. Good-Looking?

As if finally realizing they were in trouble, Axel hit the lever on the door. It swung open. She pushed him through, following him into the dark alley.

Damn it! Did no one in this area of town believe in lights?

Knowing at least four guys were behind them, she shoved Axel's back to get him moving but hit what felt like a brick wall. Her breath caught. She knew he worked out. She hadn't known he was as strong as solid steel.

He whipped around to face her. "Who are you?"

"Major Heather Larsen, Your Highness. A member of—"

"The royal guard," he said dully. "You followed me."

"You aren't as discreet as you think, and I wasn't about to lose you in my second month on the job, even if I wasn't assigned to your detail."

He snorted.

The bar door smashed open. Four men poured out.

Axel caught *her* arm. "Let's go before your boyfriend gets serious about wanting to punch one of us."

She tried to wrestle her arm free. "You've got this backward. I hustle you to safety—"

Their tussling got more physical than it should have. Royals were supposed to relax and let their guard take the lead. Instead, this guy volleyed for control.

And lost his hat.

His sleek black hair tumbled to his shoulders.

Her heart stuttered. Dear God, he was gorgeous—but, more important, with his hair loose he was recognizable.

She caught his arm again and whipped him forward, up the street. "Go! I mean it! I have to get you to safety."

He raced in front of her. "Really? *You* have to save me? Who rescued whom from the smooth operator?"

His sophisticated blunt cut hair swayed as they ran, a strange dichotomy against the ordinary clothes he wore as a disguise. But the pineapple shirt didn't hide his broad shoulders or trim waist and she'd bet her last cent the cargo shorts made his butt look amazing.

She cursed in her head, angry with herself for noticing. "I would have handled it."

"Sure. Sure."

They reached her SUV and she pointed at it. "Get in."

"I have a car."

"Someone will come for it."

The sound of the barflies barreling up the alley reached her. Suddenly, they stopped running as if they'd hit an invisible force field. Their expressions froze. Time seemed to stand still.

Finally, Mr. Good-Looking said, "Isn't that—"

Someone else said, "It's the Prince. Prince Axel."

Heather grabbed his arm again. "Get your butt in that car, right now!"

# CHAPTER TWO

THE DROP-DEAD GORGEOUS blonde opened the SUV door, shoved Prince Axel inside and was around the hood and behind the wheel in what felt like less than a second.

Heather Larson wasn't built like a pro wrestler, but she wasn't small either. Probably six feet tall, she had muscles that spoke of her strength. Her face was pretty enough to be memorable, especially with those green eyes. And that hair? Thick yellow hair to her waist. He would have remembered that.

Still, he could forgive himself for not recognizing her. Even if she had been in the castle, she'd probably been guarding his dad or his brother. Still, she'd been around for two months. If he'd seen those eyes, he was sure he would have remembered them.

Starting her car, she turned on him. "What the hell did you think you were doing?"

"What the hell do you think *you're* doing questioning a prince? The Prince who runs the department you work in by the way." He waited a beat. He was accustomed to female guards, but this one was sassier and a lot bossier than most. Absolutely not royal guard material, if only because she had no sense of dignity and decorum. The word *tomboy* came to mind, then *rebel*, then *trouble*.

"I'm pretty sure I changed some protocols when I took over Castle Admin after my dad's wedding."

"Changed protocols?"

"The ones that make sure bodyguards stay in the background."

Continuing to assess the situation, he took a long look at her. Clearly smart and strong, she eyed the area around them, assessing the situation too, but for different reasons than Axel's. He was looking at her, while she was looking at the road, choosing a route, doing her job.

All the same, she'd followed him rather than alert her supervisor and dressed down and mingled at the bar rather than announce herself to the Prince she was following. Smart or not, she didn't know a damned thing about rules or decorum.

"Any time you are guarding a member of the royal family, the situation isn't about you. You don't hide in the background and stalk your royal. You must announce yourself." He snorted. "Apparently that's a lesson you missed in orientation."

"It was an accident that I caught you sneaking out—walking up the street—to catch a cab of all things!"

"I wasn't recognized. I take great pains to make sure I'm not. I can even change my voice."

"That's fabulous. But I wasn't going to let you—"

"Let me what? Get hurt in your first few months as a guard?" He parroted what she'd said in the alley. "I wasn't going to get hurt. I've been to this bar before." He took a quick, angry breath. He used to be an ace at sneaking out. Now, a rookie guard had caught him. "Not only will I not be able to come to this bar anymore, but whoever you send for the car will know it's mine. I won't be able to use that car again."

"Buy another."

"Easy for you to say. Do you know how much trouble it is for me to hide a car? Not just the purchase itself but somewhere to store it so no one can find it—" He shook his head. "Never mind."

"I'll tell you what. I'll be the one who gets your car. I'll leave my car at the palace, take a rideshare to the bar and drive your car to that garage where you picked it up. Just give me the keys to the car and the garage and I'll take care of it. I'll even walk back to the palace, so no one knows where I've been."

That almost soothed him. The walk from his rented garage to the castle was two miles. Not so far that she'd be exhausted, but enough that he could consider it a time out for her ignoring protocol. "Fine."

"But don't expect me to apologize for keeping you safe."

He faced the window. Her speed slowed as they neared the castle. He'd gone out to blow off steam. He hadn't nearly begun to relax. The need to resign his job still tingled along his nerve endings. But here he was, back home again.

"I was okay. As I said, I've been there before, and I can handle myself."

She sniffed. "Right."

Indignation and insult rattled through him. His father thought his position nothing but details. His brother didn't even see that much. And now a guard showed him no respect?

He decided the two-mile walk wasn't going to cut it. She did not belong in the royal guard. He would have to fire her. There was no more need for conversation.

She stopped her car at the family's private entrance. After providing her with the necessary keys, he got out, closed the car door and walked into the castle.

His nerves jangling with confusion and anger, he headed to the first-floor den, flicked on the lights and walked behind the wet bar. He poured himself three fingers of bourbon and dropped down on a fussy sofa near a wall of French doors that looked out over the first garden.

"What are you doing here?"

He turned to glance behind him to see Liam standing in the entry to the den, frowning at him.

"And dressed like a...*tourist*? Good God, you have a very low regard for tourists."

Axel laughed in spite of his mood. He loved his brother... He loved his father. He knew neither had meant to make him feel irrelevant.

But they had, and for some reason or another, he couldn't shrug that off.

Liam walked to the bar. "I'm sorry about what I said before. I was just...well, furious with Dad."

"I get it." But the things his dad and brother had said had come out so easily, so naturally, that they felt like the truth. Their dismissal of his work rolled off their tongues like something they believed so much as a matter of course that it hadn't even crossed their minds not to say it.

Which had him rethinking his entire life.

Because maybe they were right. He updated procedures and protocols. He revamped departments. Fired bad employees. Hired stellar employees as replacements.

Maybe he'd done everything he could? Maybe his work in Castle Admin was done?

Obviously assuming their little disagreement was over, Liam said, "I take it you were sneaking out again."

Given that Axel was the one who taught Liam how to sneak out without getting caught, he wasn't surprised his brother had guessed. "I was. Until one of our bodyguards caught me."

Liam snorted. "You've trained them well."

"This one isn't trained at all." He took a drink of his whiskey. "And it wasn't funny. She followed me to a bar where I knew I wouldn't be recognized, basically shoved me out the emergency exit and outed me."

"What did she say to out you?"

"She didn't *say* anything. She just kept pushing me around until my hat fell off and my hair got exposed."

Liam's laugh became a guffaw. "I'd have paid to see that."

"I found it neither appropriate nor amusing. The woman's a menace."

"Really? Then how'd she become a guard?"

He raised his bourbon glass to Liam. "That's my point. She shouldn't be a guard. I have no idea why Russ hired her."

Liam frowned. "Who is she?"

"Heather Larson."

Liam's face brightened. "Heather!" His smile became a frown. "You don't like *Heather*?"

"No."

"She's the best! Dad and Rowen love her. Especially the way she is with the kids," he said, referring to his father and Rowan's eighteen-month-old twins.

"*Dad* loves her?" His plan to fire her suddenly shifted to shaky ground. No matter what Liam or Axel's roles in Prosperita were, their dad was *King.* Whenever possible, he got his own way. Nobody messed with him. Not because he was a hard-ass king, but because he was a hardworking king who deserved to have things the way he wanted them.

Maybe this was another sign that Axel wasn't serving in the right capacity. Up to this point, he'd thought he'd been doing a stellar job. Suddenly, he was questioning everything.

"Look. I get that you might have needed a break, but Dad's not going to understand it. If he finds out you went to a tourist bar, he won't be happy. My suggestion to you is to keep all this to yourself and hope Heather doesn't share the story with the other guards."

"She has to write a report."

Liam downed his bourbon. "Does she? You said she followed you out, didn't alert her supervisor. Maybe if you're nice to her, you can get her to keep it your little secret."

He headed for the door but stopped suddenly and faced Axel again. "And, just a thought, but presents usually go a long way when you're trying to get someone to do you a favor."

He left and Axel scowled at his bourbon. It

would be a cold, frosty day in hell before he'd reward bad behavior with a present. Especially to a guard who was technically under his command.

But wasn't that the point? Maybe he'd chosen the wrong capacity in which to serve his country and his King? Or maybe he'd given up what should be a life of leisure and fun, thinking he needed to serve his King and country when there wasn't really a place for him to do that?

Heather woke Tuesday morning to the ping of a message notification on her phone. She groggily groped for the little black rectangle, hit the message button and listened to her direct supervisor tell her she needed to get into the office *now*.

She winced. Clearly, he'd read her report about Prince Axel going to the den of iniquity and he was mad.

Unfortunately, though Russell Krajewski might not agree with what the Prince had done, the bigger issue was that she hadn't followed protocol. As Prince Axel had pointed out, she should have contacted her supervisor, not tailed a *prince* to a bar—without a partner. She'd actually broken a couple of rules. She hadn't alerted her supervisor. She hadn't taken another guard with her. She hadn't told Prince Axel she was there to guard him.

Her eyes popped open. *Russ was going to fire her.*

Worse, she was late. She needed to shower and dress and drive forty minutes to the castle.

*To be fired?*

She paused, wondering what the point was of racing to the castle only to be told to pack her things and leave—

Unless Russ wasn't going to fire her, just reprimand her, reminding her she should have called him when she realized Axel was sneaking out? Of course, by then Axel would have been long gone and they never would have found him.

The memory of Maryanne Montgomery separating from the group of congressional representatives Heather was guarding in Afghanistan flittered through her brain. She could still hear the ring of the shot. Still see Maryanne's face register confusion for a split second before she fell.

She took a breath to force the memory away. Losing Maryanne Montgomery was why she never, ever, ever let a client separate from a group. People who veered off on their own always got into trouble. Some died. When she'd seen the Prince leaving, she'd acted instinctively—done what she should have done when Maryanne slipped away—

That was beside the point. The rules said she was to contact her supervisor and take another guard with her when she went off script as she had the night before. They also said she was to alert the Prince that she was in the bar, that she'd followed him and she'd be guarding him.

She took a breath. She wasn't a fan of reprimands, but she deserved this one. She'd suck it up, listen to her boss and apologize, in the hope that a little contrition could help her keep the job she loved. There were plenty of royals to guard. After their dustup, *Prince Axel* probably wouldn't want her on his detail, but there was always the King, his wife, their twins, Prince Liam and the King's parents.

Plenty of people to guard.

She jumped out of bed, hopping out of her pajama bottoms as she made her way to the newly remodeled bathroom of her remote cabin. She loved the wooden beams of the high ceilings and rustic fireplaces of her house, but there were some things she wanted new and shiny. So she'd put in a modern kitchen and bath. Now her home was the oasis she'd always wanted. Ten acres of grass and trees gave her space and privacy.

After five years of feeling adrift after her divorce from her cheating husband, she'd finally found a home—or created it. No cheating, lying people allowed. No people who tell her she'll never amount to anything—

Except maybe Prince Axel. Though she'd gone above and beyond the call of duty when she'd followed him, he had not been impressed. Probably because she'd ruined his fun.

A vision of him playing pool, winking at the waitress in short shorts and losing his hat running from the barflies popped into her thoughts, and she laughed. Really laughed. The guy dripped good looks. And that body? He was perfection. Especially when he spoke. What a voice! So what if he was a charmer with the waitress? He really had been having a good time. There was a part of her that hated that she'd spoiled his fun. He looked like a guy who needed a night out—

Her eyes widened.

Oh, no! She liked him! She could understand being attracted to him. He was gorgeous. But *liking* him? Even empathizing with him? Those were wrong. Empathizing was an automatic lapse in judgment that she could fix. But they'd only spent twenty minutes together. She couldn't *like* him. No. She *didn't* like him. A charming prince who yelled at her for doing her duty? No. Just no. They were enemies.

Her shower done, she dressed, made a thermos of coffee in her modern teal, white and gray kitchen and grabbed a muffin on her way out the door.

Forty minutes later, she sat on a wooden bench in the reception area for Russell Krajewski's offices, thinking how different this space was than her cabin. The room was sophisticatedly intimidating with wooden deacon's benches painted a sharp black, and no pillows or cushions to soften the seating. Portraits of kings and queens from a century ago lined the stark white walls. Shiny marble floors with no rugs sparkled in the morning sun that poured in through the wall of windows that looked out on the guardhouse of the main gates. Literally, no one got on the palace grounds that the head of security didn't see.

That was one of the things she liked about Prosperita. They really did have a castle with a king and scrolls of traditions that provided wonderful pomp and circumstance. Living and working here was like being part of something bigger than herself, part of history.

"Ms. Larson?" Emily Grant, Russ's secretary, poked her head into the reception area. "Mr. Krajewski will see you now."

Praying they at least gave her severance pay, she took a breath, pasted a smile on her face and rose to follow Emily to his office.

A short, stocky man with a head of red hair that was turning brown and gray with age, Russ looked up from his work.

"Heather." He motioned to a chair. "Please sit down. I promise this won't take long.

"Your report threw me for a loop. The only thing stopping me from reporting Prince Axel's behavior to his dad is the fact that there seems to be no repercussions because you acted so quickly. Meaning, we will be keeping this quiet. You speak of this to no one."

Relief and confusion rattled through her. If she was being asked to keep a secret, she wasn't being fired. "Sure. Gladly."

"I'm also assigning you to his detail."

Her relief disappeared. Her confusion tripled. "That's not a good idea."

"I think it is. Prince Axel used to pull stunts like this when he was a kid. We'd thought he'd stopped but apparently not. Either way, you're the first person to catch him. I don't know if it's because you were in the right place at the right time, or if your stint in the military gives you an edge, but I want you watching him. Like a hawk."

Her face scrunched. "A hawk, sir?"

"I have a virtually unblemished record on this job and one of these days one of his stunts is going to ruin it. I retire in six months. I do not want him screwing up my record." He leaned back in his chair. "You're going to prevent that."

"Wouldn't I be better guarding the King or maybe Prince Liam since Prince Axel is already mad at me for ruining his fun?"

Russell Krajewski chortled. "I bet he is. He's going to know I put you on his detail to watch him and that will stop his shenanigans. You can handle a little bit of his anger." He glanced down at his paperwork. "That's all. Report to Gina Fulton for a new schedule."

Dumbfounded, she rose. This was not good. The Prince was already mad at her for spoiling his night. Plus, he'd know, as Russ said, that she'd been assigned to his detail specifically because she understood his antics.

She sighed heavily as she walked into the main corridor. She couldn't quit. She'd bought property in a foreign country. She had a mortgage and a remodeled kitchen and bathroom.

She walked to Gina Fulton's office and Gina gave her a new schedule, which had her reporting to Prince Axel's office that morning. She frowned at it.

She was literally starting *right now.*

*Maybe she could hide in corners? Stand behind the other guards? Oh, who was she kidding? She was six feet tall. There were a few guys she could hide behind, but not everybody.*

She headed to the executive wing.

The senior member of Axel's detail, Ron Wilson, was expecting her. "He's in his office. Working. All we have to do is watch this hall. In fact, most of the time when he's in his office we stand by this door. We only go into his office when he calls us in."

*Okay. That worked for her.*

She nodded and took her place on the left side of the open door that led to Prince Axel's assistant's office. Standing parallel to the door, she could see both the corridor in front of her and the office of Axel's support staff. Ron could see the corridor behind her and inside the support staff area.

She scanned the hall, making mental notes of places to keep an eye on. But otherwise, the area was nearly silent. Which was normal. Bodyguard work was a lot of standing around waiting for something terrible to happen, even as you prayed nothing would.

Prince Axel stepped out of his office, on his way to his secretary's desk with a handful of papers. When he saw her guarding the corridor outside his suite of offices, his eyes narrowed, then filled with fire.

He marched over to her. "Are you lost, Ms. Larson?"

Normally, guards didn't speak. But if a royal addressed them directly—and use of her name was definitely a direct address—then they *had to* reply.

"No, Prince Axel. I'm right where I'm supposed to be."

His eyes narrowed further, but Ron, clueless to the tension between them, said, "She's a new guard assigned to your detail, sir."

He stood fuming at her for a few seconds. Unlike last night's outfit, he wore a soft gray crew neck sweater, which his blunt-cut black hair skimmed at the shoulder.

Her heart thrummed, her attraction alive and well. But she reminded herself she didn't *like* him. At all. Except his looks and she'd have to be blind not to like those.

Finally, he said, "I think you and I need to chat."

His voice was as smooth as butter, with the

kind of accent that skipped over a woman's skin and gave her goosebumps. High cheekbones and a strong chin made his face perfect. His eyes were so dark and clear they seemed to be able to look into a person's soul.

Her tongue stuck to the roof of her mouth. All her good intentions about not liking him went up in smoke.

Suddenly, everything about their situation clicked in her brain. He had a way of looking at her that just melted her. *That* was the reason she'd softened to him enough that morning that she had confused *attraction* with *liking*. He had charisma that just wouldn't quit.

Which meant she didn't *like* him. All this was simply hormones. Still, they were some damned powerful hormones.

He pointed past his secretary. "Come with me."

She followed him into his office. Closing the door behind them, he walked around the desk, motioning for her to take one of the seats in front of it.

She sat, glad to be off her wobbly legs.

"You filed a report on what happened last night."

She searched for and found her voice. "Of course, I did. You sniped at me for not following protocol. I wasn't going to break another rule."

"I would have thought that having to sneak back to the bar to get my car and hide it in my private garage would have been a clue for you that we should keep last night to ourselves."

"Not a chance, now that I know what a stickler you are about rules and protocol."

Shaking his head, he leaned back in his chair.

"But you'll be happy to know that Russ said the report's going no further than his office. Your secret's safe. He doesn't want anything to ruin his nearly spotless record in his last six months as head of security."

"Then why are you here, suddenly on my detail?"

"Russ seems to think my experience makes me extra alert and you won't be able to sneak out, which further ensures his good record."

Axel scowled. "Your experience is in a war."

Discomfort skittered through her. She had considered that he'd read her file but dismissed it. After that last comment, it was pretty clear he had.

Her past and Maryanne Montgomery floated up again.

"My main job was guarding visiting dignitaries and politicians—all of whom came with staff," she reminded him. "Do you know how vigilant you have to be to guard a bunch of people who have only seen war on network TV or in movies and don't understand that you have to watch every step you make?"

* * *

Her impassioned rebuttal made Axel sit up again. Russ was right. Her training did make her super alert. He wouldn't be sneaking out on her watch.

He studied her for a second. In the light of day, she wasn't just pretty. She was stunning. Her green eyes glittered with fire. Her thick hair might be in a ponytail, but he knew it reached her waist.

Feelings he'd squelched the night before sparked to life. He told himself that she was an employee, and he couldn't be attracted to her.

Well, technically, that wasn't true. He *could* be attracted to her. He simply couldn't do anything about it.

Which was for the best. The woman was a menace.

He rose. "That's all."

"Are you sure? You're not going to set up a bunch of rules or protocols for me to follow since you think I'm a lightweight guard?"

He almost laughed. Her impertinence should make him furious. Instead—maybe because he'd met her the night before under odd circumstances and they'd established a weird relationship—he wanted to laugh.

He wouldn't. "No. I do not have extra rules or protocols for you." A thought came to mind, and he hid a snicker. "But just remember. The same way you're watching me, I'll be watching you."

Finally realizing he was dismissing her, she rose. But she caught his gaze. "Careful, Your Highness. I'm liable to think you have a crush on me."

"I—I do not have a crush on you!" He hated that that sentence came out on a sputter. Grown men did not have crushes. He might want to sleep with her, but he didn't have a crush.

Maybe he should tell her that? Maybe it would stop the far too free way she spoke to him?

No. Too risky. He had no idea how she'd reply. She wasn't a normal guard. Hell, in some respects she wasn't a normal woman.

Of course, what *was* a normal woman—

He stopped himself from thinking any further. Good God. His thought processes went haywire when she was around.

"You're dismissed."

She angled her thumb behind her. "I'll be right outside the door if you think of a rule I need."

She left and he waited until the door was closed securely behind him to growl with frustration. He'd be talking to Russ about the way she spoke to him. He might even try to use it to get her off his detail. But Russ was a bulldog. If his intention really was to keep Axel in line to preserve his stellar reputation as head of security, especially for the last six months of his career, then nothing would change his mind.

That brought the whole quitting-his-job-and-going-back-to-being-a-rebel plan into his thoughts. If he couldn't even sneak out to get a break to think, how was he going to make a good decision? Of course, he'd sneaked out of the palace the whole way through his teens and most of his twenties. He had a mind for finding loopholes and lapses in security. He could get those skills back.

He'd simply have to make sure Heather Larson wasn't on duty the nights he wanted to leave.

He also would have to stop talking to her, stop giving her openings to be sassy.

And not laugh when she said something silly.

And not notice all that pretty hair or those seductive eyes.

He frowned.

Of all the wrenches to be thrown into his life, a stunning, overzealous guard was the one he'd least expected. Of course, if he quit his job and went back to simply being the rebel Prince, he wouldn't be sneaking out of the castle. He'd be sneaking out of hotels or going to casinos as a matter of course. He wouldn't need to worry about an overzealous guard.

What an odd choice. Quit his job and go back to being frivolous, a guy who existed to have fun. Or stay where he was, heading up Castle Admin, knowing that what he did went unnoticed by the very people he was protecting.

Buffeted by confusion, he couldn't sit in his office anymore. He did some of his best thinking on the track, and with this situation weighing so heavily on his mind, he wouldn't get any other work done. Might as well take a run.

He walked into his private bathroom suite, changed into sweatpants and a T-shirt and left through a concealed door in the corridor to the right of his office.

# CHAPTER THREE

HEATHER WAS STANDING across the hall from Ron when he tapped his earpiece and said, "Got it. Thanks, Russ."

"What?"

"The Prince is on the running track," Ron explained.

She frowned. The grounds were fenced in. There were cameras everywhere. Guards were scattered around and where there weren't guards, there were cameras.

With no order from Russ to follow him, it was clear he wasn't worried. Still—

Did *she* want to take the chance that he had a car stashed behind a bush and could be out of sight in the time it took to unlock a gate? Particularly when she had basically been told it was her job to stay one step ahead of him?

He was going to hate this, but she'd seen what happened when someone broke protocol and went off on their own.

She sighed and faced Ron. "We have to follow

him. I've seen his work. Don't make me explain. But trust me. We don't want to stand down. He's a flight risk."

Not knowing about the Prince's little side trip the night before, Ron frowned. "He is?"

"Yes. Stay here if you want. But I'm going to change clothes and stick to him like butter on hot toast."

Ron cursed. "I'll watch him until you change."

"Good plan."

He ran outside. She hurried to the locker room. As she'd done the night before, she took off her jacket and white shirt, leaving her baby blue tank top. She switched her dress slacks for shorts and had tennis shoes on her feet before she ran out to the track.

Twenty feet behind the Prince, Ron stopped running when he saw her. She waved him off, letting him know that he and his probably stiflingly hot black suit could get out of the heat and go back inside. Then she jogged up to Axel.

"Nice morning for a run."

He sighed when he saw her. "So now I can't even get a little exercise?"

The memory of Maryanne Montgomery rose again. The loss had broken her for weeks. It was the reason she'd followed Axel out of the castle the night before, the reason she'd written her report, the reason she didn't take any of his lip with regard to her duties. She would never go through that again.

But she also wouldn't explain that to the guy she was protecting. He'd read her file. He knew her past. If he couldn't put two and two together, she wouldn't spell out four.

"Nope. I'm not about to break a rule or miss a protocol."

"I should have just gone to the gym."

Keeping up with his easy pace, she glanced around at the leafy trees, the blue sky, the neatly manicured grounds with flowering plants in groupings every hundred yards or so. "Shame to be indoors on a day like this."

He snorted.

"Besides, I would have followed you to the gym and stuck by your side."

"Fabulous."

"You know, you're angry about this, but you started it. You're the one who snuck out, making us realize you're not trustworthy. Then you were the one who mentioned protocols. You made me feel I have to be on my toes a hundred percent."

He sighed.

"You can't blame me."

"I suppose I can't."

His far too easy acquiescence caused her brow to wrinkle. "Don't agree with me! It makes me think you're planning something." She looked around. "The fence is too high for you to climb.

Of course, you could have a car hidden by one of the gates."

He groaned. "I do not have a car hidden by one of the gates! I took a cab yesterday, remember?"

"See. There you go again. You might have said that to throw me off track."

He gaped at her. "Are you going to distrust everything I say?"

"Probably. Misdirection is the easiest way to get away with things."

He shook his head. "At some point you have to trust me."

"I don't think so."

He groaned again.

"Might as well get used to me, being right here, at your side."

Frustrated, he stared at her. No one looked better in baby blue than a blonde. The color did amazing things for her skin tone and made her green eyes appear greener. He hadn't yet found a way to get a peek at her legs, but he was sure they were perfect. Everything else about her was.

The only problem was he wasn't allowed to notice. Not only that, but she was also destroying his think time. How could he sort out his job—his future—with her jibber jabbering beside him?

Worse, she was clever in the same devious way he was. She would always be one step ahead of him.

"I'll bet you were hell on wheels in school."

She laughed. "Nope. I was the quiet one. It was at home where I had to be on my toes. I had five brothers and no sisters. They played practical jokes on me until I got smart enough to return the favor. Then I got better at pranks than they were, and I ruled the house."

He snickered. "I did about the same thing to my brother, Liam."

"Liam!" She gaped at him. "He's such a nice guy! How could you torment him!"

"Ech. He was an easy mark, and I was bored."

They rounded the track for the second time, two miles, and he stopped and put his hands on his knees to catch his breath. "That's it for this morning. For the record, I'll walk back into my office area through the corridor behind that door—" He pointed at the wooden door set discreetly in the stone. "Then I'll go directly to my private bathroom and shower before I put my clothes on again." He waggled his eyebrows. "Want to watch?"

Her face reddened. "No. I do not want to watch. But *for the record,* I won't always believe you when you tell me where you're going. Don't think you'll establish a pattern of trust by doing what you said you were going to do a few times, so I'll start trusting you and then you can sneak out."

"I wouldn't—"

She stopped him with a wave of her hand. "Five brothers, remember? I'll never trust you."

With that she walked away, then turned and motioned for him to join her. She, literally, intended to walk him to the entry.

She really wasn't ever going to trust him. If he wanted privacy to think this through, he'd probably have to stay in his bathroom.

He worked the rest of the day, occasionally turning his chair to face the castle grounds to take a minute or two to ponder his life and the choices before him, but mostly he read reports on departmental efficiency.

He left his office at little after four o'clock, expecting another run-in with Heather when he entered the corridor outside his door, but she wasn't there. Two fresh guards stood sentry. Considering that eight hours had gone by, he assumed she was off duty and though he said goodnight to the guards who had replaced her and Ron, he said nothing else.

He had a snack in his quarters, took a short nap and then dressed for an outing. His father and his wife, Rowan, loved art galleries, and this evening they were hosting a fundraiser for the local children's hospital. Axel and Liam were required to attend. But that was good. Considering that he was on the precipice of leaving his job, he could look at his life like an observer. See if he really didn't mind being tied down to Prosperita, or if he'd merely accepted it in the name of doing the job he thought his family needed.

Of course, if he went with this logic, then he'd have to look at the other side of the coin. He'd have to take a trip soon, to examine what his life *could* be. Maybe somewhere like Monaco. He could go to the casinos. Maybe meet a woman—

With a bodyguard by his side?

Even without giving it any thought, he *knew* Russ would send Heather with him, and she'd watch every damned move he made.

He'd have to learn to ignore her.

He *would* ignore her. The whole point of thinking through his life was to get the real experience of what his life would be like if he resigned as head of Castle Admin. A bodyguard would be part of that.

Dressed in his tux, he jogged down the dramatic stairway of the castle's main entry. A guard opened the ornate double doors for him.

He said, "Thank you," and all but skipped out into the warm night. Just the thought of going to Monaco for a few days had put the spring back in his step. Maybe it really was time for him to hand off the new and improved Castle Admin and go back to his wicked, wicked ways?

"Good evening, Leo."

The driver opened the door. "Good evening, sir."

His good mood restored, he said, "Beautiful night."

"Yes, sir, it is."

He slid into the limo. As he settled on the seat, he blinked. Heather sat right beside him.

"What are you doing here?"

"My job?"

"You worked all day!"

"Yeah, but Russ thought it would be a good idea for me to go with you to this event. You know? Be the thorn in your side that I've come to love being."

He would have laughed at that, but this was getting ridiculous.

"My father and stepmother planned this evening. I will not sneak out."

"There you go again, trying to get me to trust you." She laughed. "I said it before. I will say it again. Five brothers. Best training in the world."

He snorted, then accepted his fate. Head of Castle Admin or fun-loving, rebel prince, he would always have a bodyguard. He had to factor that into his decision. "Whatever."

"You don't have to worry about me spoiling your fun." She motioned to her official dark suit and white shirt. "I'm dressed to blend."

He leaned into the cushy limo seat. "You won't even eat a shrimp or two? Grab a glass of champagne?"

"If I were, would I tell my boss, the guy who heads the department I work in?"

No. She was too clever for that.

An odd respect filled him. If he distanced himself from the situation and thought of her as an employee of the most important department in Castle Admin, she was probably his best employee. If he took that one step further, looking at his behavior from the perspective of the guy in charge of keeping *him* safe, he'd have to admit he did need extra special guarding.

Especially given the weird mood he was in.

The limo grew quiet. Too quiet for a twenty-minute drive. "So...you have five brothers?"

"Yes."

"And you were the only girl?"

"I counted my mother as a girl. It was two of us against the world."

He chuckled.

"What about you? What's it like to grow up a prince?"

He couldn't tell if she disliked the silence as much as he did or if she had simply grown so familiar with him that she thought conversation between them was a natural thing. But either way, he felt like talking. He would have told her it used to be a lot of fun to be a prince until he got a guard who stuck to him like a bumper sticker, but he was tired of the unimportant back and forth. Maybe if they had a real conversation, they'd find common ground and make peace of a sort.

"Being a prince was amazing in some ways and horrid in others. When my mother died, I felt like a bug under a microscope. If I cried, the papers hinted I was weak. If I didn't cry, I had no feelings."

"Wow."

He gave her a sideways glance. Just from the tone of her voice, he could tell she understood what he was saying. But talking about that time of his life brought it back full force. The feeling of living in a fishbowl. Having his life dissected as if he were a thing, not a person. The scrutiny had taught him to hide his feelings and be the rebel Prince they loved to print about. No substance. No reality. Just fun. But over the years, he'd done such a good job of shoving down his feelings that eventually he didn't have any real emotions anymore. Which was fine considering he wouldn't expose a woman to the kind of scrutiny royals endured. That wasn't to say he didn't date. He simply kept the time he spent with a woman so short the press barely had a chance to uncover his date's name before she was off his radar.

The realization of how shallow his life had become washed over him, and he wondered if that wasn't part of his sudden discontent—

It didn't matter. He'd keep this conversation light, friendly, because that was what he did. That was how he survived.

"I know, right? I was a teenager who became fodder for the press. Worst thing I've ever gone through. It made me grow up fast."

"If your behavior after that is any clue, it also seemed to make you not care what anyone said."

He snickered at her perception. She might not totally understand life as a royal, but she figured out the bottom line. "True."

The limo grew quiet again. He took a breath. Now it was her turn. She'd been to war. She'd survived being the only girl in a big family. If they were going to find common ground and make peace, he had to hear about her too.

He peeked at her. "Tell me about *your* childhood."

"I didn't have the press following my every move so I could torment my brothers to my heart's content."

He laughed. "I know that's a large part of who you are, but surely there's more."

When she said nothing, he groaned. "Come on. I trust you with my life. Literally. And I told you about the worst thing that happened to me."

She sighed. "All right, if you're balancing the scales by asking me to tell you something of equal importance to what you told me, I'd have to say losing Maryanne Montgomery was the worst thing in my life."

Having read her file, he knew she was talking about the death of a person in a detail she was protecting. He sat back, surprised she'd taken him literally, but oddly pleased that she trusted him enough to really share. "The assistant to the congressman?"

She nodded. "Diplomats are accustomed to bodyguards, following orders and keeping a low profile. Their staffs are focused on doing their jobs, being one step ahead of their boss. They might wear a vest and a helmet, but they scurry around, fall out of formation. Half the time I don't think they even pay attention to orders. They're always on their phones."

"You were cleared of any wrongdoing."

"I know." She looked down at her hands. "But that doesn't bring Maryanne back."

"She made her choices."

She snorted. "Which is why I won't let you make yours."

He knew she was trying to lighten the mood again, but he could see the regret in her serious green eyes. In that second, she wasn't a member of his detail or even a gorgeous woman. She was a person who'd suffered a horrible loss.

Silence once again filled the limo. She'd taken her own kind of beating in the press. It was no wonder they empathized with each other.

The urge to take her hand and let her feel his understanding swamped him. He fought it. They weren't friends—

But he suddenly realized he'd like to be. There was a depth about her that most men probably didn't see. She wasn't like anybody he'd ever met. Not to mention that she was beautiful.

The inside of the limo warmed with intimacy.

Attraction hit him in a wave of longing for something he'd never even known existed, let alone considered for himself and his life. What would it be like to be totally honest with someone? To express his feelings without reserve and not just be the Prince the press portrayed him to be?

The very idea floored him. Squelching his feelings was how he stayed safe—

A profound thought hit him. *This* was what his father had found with Rowan. An equal. Someone he could be his honest self with. He'd seen it every day since his dad met the current Queen, but he'd never put it together until now.

They reached the gallery. Leo pulled up to the entrance. A valet opened the limo door. Axel slid out, recognizing the valet as one of the royal guard—another thing he'd done to improve security. Guards filled simple positions like waiter or valet, watching for trouble, protecting his dad and brother.

Pleased with his work, but a little sad that what he did made no impression on the very people he protected, the odd feeling of insignificance filled him again, except now it was compounded by the shallowness of his life. Trying to ignore it, he reached inside, extending his hand to help

Heather out of the back seat. As she took it, their eyes met. His chest tightened with something he could neither define nor describe. Everything he felt about his job, his place in the world, the shallowness of his life, faded away into nothing. Something unique and wonderful filled him. Longing for more of it bathed him in a need to hold on to it, to explore it.

Was this how his dad's feelings for Rowan had started? With a longing for a real life only she'd ever shown him?

Heather stepped out, onto the street, and he let go of her hand. Two other guards from his detail walked him to the door. Heather stayed behind.

He felt it like a loss, but he also knew the drill. He smiled and waved at reporters as his picture was taken hundreds of times. The gallery door opened for him. The whir of cameras welcomed him inside.

He smiled broadly, bussing a kiss on his stepmother's cheek. Queen Rowan looked amazing with her gorgeous red hair arranged in a fancy hairdo on top of her head and her strapless purple gown.

His father and Rowan had some kind of joke about purple gowns that they'd never shared, and he suddenly envied their closeness. The emptiness of his life poured through him again. His father and brother didn't understand what he did, the place he'd carved out for himself. His mother was gone. Not that he didn't love Rowan as a step-parent. She was an easy person to love. Warm and affectionate, she brought life into their little family again. His half-brother and sister were like gifts from God.

But no matter how picture-perfect his life looked, the thing he'd worked to avoid since his mother's passing was manifesting.

He was alone.

# CHAPTER FOUR

HEATHER TOOK A quick breath as Prince Axel disappeared into the art gallery. She'd thought telling him about Maryanne Montgomery would be a simple thing, since he already knew from reading her file. Plus, it really was balancing her end of the conversation with what he'd told her.

But telling him had felt like sharing a confidence with a trusted friend. That didn't merely strike her oddly because she did not trust him—couldn't trust him—but he was royalty. How could they be friends? What could they possibly have in common?

More than that, though, she normally wasn't attracted to gorgeous guys and Prince Axel was beyond gorgeous. He was dark, brooding and so sexy, her whole body vibrated when he was around.

Still, from a twenty-minute conversation in a limo, she knew something troubled him. Her instinct had been to let him talk about losing his mom when he was a teenager, but he'd shifted the conversation to her. Before they could take the conversation back to him, they'd arrived at the gallery, and he'd exited the limo.

But he'd turned to offer his hand to help her out and she'd taken it. Electricity hadn't zapped up her arm. Something more, something warmer, had. Intimacy had arched between them. Was that because he'd told her about his mom, and she'd told him her greatest sorrow? Or because they understood each other?

Whatever it was, she would have to steer clear of those kinds of conversations with him. She'd also have to stop noticing how handsome he was, how deep his thoughts, how strong he was to handle it all.

Shaking her head, she took her fifteen-minute break by using the restroom and drinking a bottle of water. As if he'd been watching the time, Russ ambled over to her.

"Eddie Farnsworth is due to go off duty. You're his replacement. He's against the back wall in the main exhibit room."

Having gone over the blueprint with the team late that afternoon, Heather nodded and went inside, using a private door that was guarded by two of her peers. Walking along a wall, it was easy to fade into the background. She found Eddie and took his place, blending, the way a good guard did.

She stood at her post for almost three hours, wondering how long this event would last. A quick glance told her the King and Queen were having a wonderful time, laughing and talking with attendees, most of whom seemed to be good friends. Sometimes Axel was in their circle, laughing, talking when appropriate, but she saw a distance between him and his dad and stepmom, between him and Liam. Telling herself to stop noticing, she scanned the room again.

Russ ambled over, giving her another break. Glad for a chance to get away, she headed outside. The gallery was on a lake. Just beyond the door was a park, with benches that looked out over the water. She walked to the park, intending to take her fifteen minutes sitting on a bench, but saw a wrought iron fence and couldn't resist.

Leaning against it, she took a deep breath of the damp air.

"I thought you were supposed to be watching me."

Hearing Axel's voice, she laughed, then caught herself. She wasn't supposed to be happy to see him. He leaned against the fence beside her.

"There are tons of guards in there. You're fine."

"Not worried I'm going to sneak out?"

"You like your stepmother too much to do that."

He smirked. "I told you."

"Yeah. You did."

"We do sort of veer off into real conversations."

"No. When you told me that you were trying to convince me you didn't need a guard."

He laughed, then took a deep breath of the air as she had. "The event should be over soon."

She rotated her shoulders to relieve their stiffness. "Good. I could use a beer."

"You could sneak one."

She eyed him. "I'm not you. I'll wait till I'm off duty."

"Meaning, I couldn't tempt you with another trip to the bar where we met?"

She almost choked on a laugh. "No."

The conversation died, but they were now facing each other, casually leaning against the fence, like two friends.

"Why the hell do you have to be so beautiful?"

Pleasure rippled through her at the unexpected compliment. Still, she didn't let it show on her face or in her voice. "My mother's genes. Why the hell did you have to be so handsome?"

"My father's genes." He blew his breath out on a long sigh. "It's such a bad thing for us to be attracted to each other."

After what happened when he helped her out of the limo, she couldn't pretend she didn't know what he was talking about. She snorted. "No kidding."

He stared at her, equally surprised and pleased she hadn't denied the attraction. The urge to kiss her rumbled through him. Once he acknowledged it, it grew into chest-tightening longing.

Out of respect for her, he stepped back.

She also stepped back. Her eyes softened with regret. The flash of it was so quick, he might have missed it if he hadn't been desperately searching for a sign that he wasn't crazy. That this thing that arched between them really was strong.

The desire to inch forward and kiss her blossomed in his chest again. But though he knew she felt what he felt, he also knew she wouldn't want it. Not because she wasn't attracted to him but because she was, and she wasn't allowed to be.

Technically, he wasn't allowed to be either.

Plus, he was in a horribly muddled stage of his life. At some point, she might be guarding him when he was in Paris or Monaco, wooing women. More to the point, no matter how attracted they were, he wouldn't want anything but a fling. Heather was a serious woman who would probably want something more and he didn't do "more." He had quick affairs that were over before the press could catch wind of them.

The reminder of who he really was caused him to take another step back.

He might be confused about his place in the world, but he wasn't confused about who he was. Rather than call himself shallow again, he deemed himself a free spirit who liked fun and didn't need anyone. He wasn't serious. He was light. He was the one the press would never be able to persecute or vilify. He never stayed in one place or with one woman long enough for them to get that kind of dirt on him. Or the women he spent time with. He could pretend to be a troublemaker, flirt and make the reporters laugh. But that was as far as things went. He'd been safe and a little smug over how he kept everybody at an arm's distance until he'd gone to that bar—

No. Until he'd been assigned a beautiful guard who was determined to keep him in line, but who was also the most interesting person he'd met in a long, long time—if ever.

But he wasn't allowed to pursue her. And even if he was, he would not subject her to the hounding she'd get in the media. She could be a darling one day, and a villain the next. Especially, if the press looked into her past.

And found Maryanne Montgomery.

That was the kicker. The investigation that followed the aide's death had put her through the wringer. He would not be responsible for reopening that wound.

He turned to go back into the gallery. "I'm sure I'll see you later," he called over his shoulder.

She laughed. "Maybe yes. Maybe no. I don't think I'm the person riding home in the limo with you."

Disappointment rattled through him. He ignored it then realized just how odd his life was. He couldn't kiss a woman he wanted to kiss, not merely out of worry for his own privacy, but for hers. Heather deserved to be more than the pretty girl on his arm one week and the woman he dumped the next—unless he wanted her to become fodder for the press and relive the part of her life she'd deemed as horrible as him losing his mother.

He would never be so selfish as to put her through that.

The guard opening the gallery door for him brought him back to the present. He glanced around at everyone having fun—his father, Rowan, Liam— and wondered how he could leave their care to someone else.

But was it really him who made the difference? Security might have been sketchy before he'd promoted Russ. But right now? Security was tight. Protocols were strong. His guards were the best.

Did it need to be him who steered the ship? Or had he repaired the ship well enough to know it would run smoothly even if he handed it off?

Wednesday, Prince Axel had a photo op with his stepmother and the participants in that year's Academic Excellence Competition. Standing in a discreet corner of Queen Rowan's office, watching her royal, Heather remembered the night before, the way a simple encounter had turned into curiosity about kissing Axel, and she realized how lucky she was that she was too smart to give in to feelings like that.

She could credit her lousy husband's antics for making her stop and think before she reacted, but there was a bittersweetness to that. Because she was so wise about things like getting involved with a man, she'd never again experience the joy of a surprise kiss, an unexpected kiss, a kiss that was borderline wrong—

Didn't matter. She'd given herself a good talking to after Prince Axel had returned to the gallery and another one in the shower before she went to bed.

Something had flared between them, but he'd clearly decided not to kiss her. And she knew better than to kiss him. Though they kept getting friendlier, crossing that line would get her fired. Having decided never to marry again, her career had become her life. She would do nothing to jeopardize it.

The kissing problem was sorted.

He'd said good morning to her and her counterpart when they met in the corridor to walk him to the Queen's office, but that was it. Meaning, he'd clearly come to the same conclusion she had.

Life had gone back to normal.

Though she did get a heart tug watching him interact with the adorable children from the academic competition. The projects they'd submitted for consideration ranged from picture books to scientific experiments that showed off math and physics skills. All were online, available for friends and family to see, and the winners were thrilled to be acknowledged and to meet members of the royal family.

As the Queen handed out medals, Axel shook hands with the grinning medalists, then took the podium to give a short speech on the importance of education. Heather had been around enough dignitaries to know when someone was reciting facts that had been given to them and when someone was speaking from the heart. Axel was speaking from the heart. He told everyone of the importance of knowledge and imagination for taking the world into the next century. He believed education was the way to world peace.

It was so moving and so perfect, she once again knew there was more to him than met the eye. Even as she wistfully wished she could uncover all his secrets, she knew she couldn't. She *wouldn't*. She had a life plan. One that didn't involve getting romantic with a man out of her station in life. That's what had happened with Glen. The son of the people who owned the factory that employed most of the people in her small town, he was the guy everybody had wanted to marry. When he'd chosen her, she'd worked so hard to please him—to keep him—that she'd lost herself.

That would not happen again.

She walked a foot behind Prince Axel as he returned to his office, then took her post outside his door. At noon, Russ called her into his office and told her the royal family was having dinner on their yacht that night and she should go home and get some rest because he wanted her in Axel's limo and on the yacht.

Righteous indignation for Axel fluttered through her. He wasn't being a rebel. Something was bothering him. Something that had made him feel he needed a break the night he'd sneaked out to that seedy bar. Still, she also agreed with Russ that his slipping away could be dangerous.

She accepted her orders with a nod, went home, took a nap, ate an early dinner and returned to the castle. She questioned her need to be there when she was told the royal family had all ridden to the yacht in the King's limo.

But when she boarded the yacht and was assigned to stand on the deck, she didn't care if she was needed or not. The night was warm, the inky sky filled with stars. The calm sea filled her with peace and a respite that loosened her muscles and quieted her brain. She never would have gotten to see so many wonderful things if she'd stayed in Louisiana instead of becoming a bodyguard for a royal family.

That made her heart happy as lights from the dining room poured out over part of the deck. Still, she stayed in the shadows, watching the water, looking for a dinghy or a stealthy swimmer. No matter how she phrased it, she was looking for a terrorist, keeping the wonderful family in that dining room safe.

Laughter billowed out of the open windows, and she smiled. She loved this job, but more than that she loved these people. Their roles might make their personal relationships different, even difficult, but deep down they worked to be as normal of a family as they possibly could be.

"Are guards who are lost in thought really doing their jobs?"

She stopped the smile that tried to form when she heard Axel's voice. "I was thinking about you guys, so technically I was doing my duty."

He walked over to the railing and leaned against it.

She shook her head. "You cannot tell me you're bored."

"No. It's time for me to go back to the castle. Dad, Rowan and the twins are taking the yacht farther out to enjoy a few days at sea. So it looks like you're riding back to the dock with me in a dinghy."

"I've ridden in stranger vehicles."

He laughed. "I think that's one of the things I like about you. Your life, though different, is as weird as mine."

"Or maybe I just have some unique life experiences."

"Way to pretty it up."

She laughed, making the bubble of happiness in her heart even more obvious. "I thought you said we should stop hanging out together because of our little attraction."

"I say a lot of things. Besides, I came out here to let you know we'd be leaving soon."

"And you're staying with me because…?"

He shrugged. "Something always seems to draw me to you." He caught her gaze. "Even though it's against my better judgment that tells me I'm a philanderer and you're a serious person." He motioned around the yacht. "I mean, look at your job. To me, it doesn't get any more serious than this."

"I know."

"So why is it that when I see you in the moonlight, I get tempted to want something I know I can't have?"

She swallowed hard, reminding herself she had to stop being so friendly with this guy or one of these days she'd slip up and be in trouble. But the pull of his dark eyes held her captive.

Her phone pinged with a text. She slid it out of her trouser pocket and read the text from Russ telling her what Axel had just told her. That they were leaving soon.

It was enough to bring her back to reality and she shook her head. "Come on. I know our banter is fun…but, seriously, there's absolutely no future for us and if we keep this up, one of these days we *will* slip, and *I'll* be in trouble."

"I'll take full responsibility and get you off the hook."

"You're missing the point."

"Better than missing a few minutes of fun. My family is great." He pointed to the dining room with lights now muted. "But family has a place and friends have a place."

She didn't miss the way he'd said "a few minutes of fun" and reminded herself that something troubled him.

He faced her. The moon bathed him in pale light. His voice lowered to a whisper as he said, "You're sure I can't talk you into going back to that bar, where we could just be ourselves?"

That was when she saw it. While she was feeling all kinds of connection, he liked her because she was a form of escape for him.

Disappointment tightened her chest, but it was a foolish feeling for a woman who loved her job and didn't want another relationship. "Okay. I see what you're doing but this has to end tonight."

"Like Cinderella, you'll be someone different tomorrow, so I should kiss you tonight?"

It was the last thing she expected him to say. "You shouldn't kiss me at all." But a thrill roared through her. What would it be like to kiss this incredible man? "I work for you. I'm not your bar buddy. I am protecting you."

He looked around. "From fireflies?"

She wanted to laugh—so very desperately

wanted to laugh because there was just something about him that loosened her restraints and gave her the sense that life could be fun again. That the husband who had made her feel worthless was the anomaly. That most people were kind and good.

She held back. "Very funny."

"There's no one here. No one would see if I kissed you."

She gaped at him. "Look who you're talking to. There's always someone watching you. Always someone who will see. Besides. You and me? Bad idea."

He inched closer. "Do you really think that?"

Her heart didn't. Or maybe it was her soul. Her odd marriage had left an empty place inside of her. Talking to him made it disappear. But her brain saw all the problems associated with falling for a prince, especially a prince she was guarding. Even if she was willing to give up her job for him, she'd gone through one problematic relationship. Dating a prince would be a hundred times worse.

He laughed. "Wow. You think a lot. Too much. Have you ever just let go and had fun?"

No. And *that* was the difference between him and her ex. Glen wanted her to be the pretty girl on his arm. Nothing more. Axel wanted to have fun with her, to let her be herself.

Maybe that was why Axel tempted her so much?

Her phone pinged. She glanced down at it. "Dinghy's ready."

*Thank God.*

She caught his arm to guide him to the dinghy, but he caught her arm too, forcing her to turn to him. His handsome face in shadows, he smiled at her. Their unusual intimacy arched between them. She could so easily believe he liked *her*—didn't merely see her as a form of escape—but memories of her divorce brought her to her senses. Axel might not be like her ex, but a relationship with him would be riddled with as much trouble as her marriage had been.

"Let's go."

He searched her eyes. For a second, she was sure he would say something, tease her, tempt her, but he quietly released her. When he turned away, he walked several feet in front of her, as if he'd dismissed her.

She felt the loss like a physical thing, but this was for the best.

Axel woke to the sound of his phone buzzing with a text. Feeling along his bedside table, he found it and, bleary-eyed, read the missive from his father's personal assistant.

Meeting in the King's office at nine.

It was seven o'clock. He could shower, eat and be in that wing of the castle in plenty of time. He got out of bed, not concerned with the fact that the text was from his dad's assistant. She frequently handled jobs like that—

Except the King was supposed to be on the yacht, with Rowan and the twins. He frowned, then he realized this could easily be a video meeting.

As he stepped into the shower, the situation rolled out of his thoughts but that left room for Heather to tumble in. Perhaps the part of him that liked to tease and have fun was reawakening. But even if he did decide to quit Castle Admin and go back to living to have fun, he didn't want to hurt her, or worse, cost her her job. So he would stay away from her.

Still, if she'd been receptive the night before, he would have kissed her. He knew it as well as he knew the names of everyone in his royal lineage. The moonlight had made the deck romantic, and the warm air had carried the scent of her shampoo to him on a soft breeze. Both of which made him forget the thing she remembered. There was always someone watching him.

On a frustrated curse, he wished for a day, an hour, even a few minutes of complete privacy for them to be themselves when they could—

He didn't let himself finish the thought because he knew that would unleash hormones that might follow him around all day. Besides, it was wrong. There would never be a time they'd be totally alone.

Never.

There was no point wishing for it.

He left his apartment, walked to the family dining room—which he found empty—and answered a few emails on his phone as he ate his breakfast.

Then he headed to the executive wing and his dad's office. He entered to see Russ and Heather were already there, sitting on the two chairs in front of his father's desk. Even in the nondescript black suit and white shirt, with her hair in a ponytail, she looked spectacular, enticing.

But he couldn't have her. No more pointless meanderings.

When Russ saw Axel enter, he rose and relinquished his seat. "Sit here, Prince Axel."

He frowned. As he sat, Heather seemed to shrink away from the chair, as if she were worried that something about their body language would give away their unusual relationship, reminding him to be on his best behavior...*for her*. She was the one who would lose if they slipped up. He would protect her. Even from himself.

Suddenly, the side door opened and his dad entered.

He, Heather and Russ rose out of respect and protocol, but the King waved them back down again.

Axel didn't have time to ponder his dad's appearance when he was supposed to be on a yacht before the King said, "Good morning."

Everyone responded with "Good morning, Your Majesty."

His dad motioned to the open office door with his chin and Russ walked over and closed it.

His dad said, "We have a situation."

Axel's heart scurried with fear—he, the head of Castle Admin, was in a meeting with the King, the head of security and probably the best guard they had.

Something was really wrong.

Russ leaned against the corner of the King's desk. Axel recognized the intimacy of it, as if Russ and his father were coconspirators.

Which ramped up his fear. Why would his dad—or even Russ—bypass him to form a plan? What the hell was going on?

The King continued, "Last night Security intercepted a death threat."

Axel's heart stopped. He thought the threat was to his dad—except Russ would have run that by him, not his father. Which meant this threat was on someone else's life and had some teeth. Some real teeth. Or they wouldn't be here.

"The threat is to your life, Axel."

"Mine?" His thoughts muddled with a confusion that drove out his fear. He was a spare prince. Not the member of the royal family who got death threats. "Really?"

His father leaned forward, resting his arms on the desk in front of him. "It seems your foray into the bar scene on the bad side of town got some attention."

*Oh, damn.* The threat might not have teeth as much as it shone a light on him sneaking out. Which was probably why Heather was here. To make sure he told the truth about what had happened that night.

"You were recognized when your hat fell off. The email contained a photo of the hat, more or less as proof that you really were at the bar and this man who made the threat really had seen you."

"I can explain…"

"Why you were there is now irrelevant. The threat is what concerns us. It's barebones." His father picked up a piece of paper and began reading. *"Stay where you belong, or you will be sorry."* He glanced at Axel again. "But barebones or not we're taking it seriously."

Not sure what was going on, if he was being reprimanded or if his dad was angry that he'd attracted unwanted attention, Axel straightened in his chair. "We take all threats seriously."

"Yes, we do," his father agreed. "But a preliminary investigation by Russ this morning told us that the IP account from which the threat was sent belongs to a man who is a former member of the military." He caught Axel's gaze again. "Who got a dishonorable discharge for making threats against his superior officer."

"He's a hothead," Russ put in. "And the thing about hotheads is you never know when the big talk is going to turn into action."

Axel took a second to process that. Russ had gone to his dad to cover his own butt because he knew Axel had sneaked out but hadn't reported it. His dad, though angry, wanted to handle the threat properly—just in case.

It was how security worked. A smart organization ran down every threat, every potential problem.

"Okay. I get it. You want me to curtail my activities for a few days or weeks while we work through this."

"No," King Jozef said, sitting back in his chair. "This is a big week for you. You have two personal appearances."

"If you suddenly back out," Russ said, "the man who sent the threat could think he scared us, which could embolden him. Bragging about how he scared you into hiding might make him feel cocky enough to send another threat."

Axel looked at Russ, then his dad. "What are you saying?"

Russ said, "We're saying we believe this guy is nothing more than a hothead drunk who will wake up sorry he sent that email—if he even remembers he sent it—and he'll pray no one arrests him. That's what we hope."

"Okay."

*That was what usually happened.*

"But this one could just as easily go the other way."

His dad cut in. "So you'll have more protection than usual, just in case."

Axel nodded.

His dad smiled. "Including the very capable Ms. Larson at your side."

Axel took a moment to let everything sink in. It sounded like business as usual to him. Precautions while they ran down everything they could on the sender. Not wanting to make a bigger deal out of it than it needed to be—while they kept an eye on this guy and gathered intel.

"Okay."

"Don't be so flippant," Russ said. "Most of our threats come from ordinary people, disgruntled with something, blaming the King. This one came to you, from someone who had contact with you. Heather's report talked about a guy who was flirting with her, and you yanked him away."

Axel grimaced.

The King said, "You know contact like that gives a threat a different kind of meaning."

He did know. In a way, he'd picked a fight with that guy.

"Or the person who sent the email might not be

the one you tussled with," Russ said. "The only name we have is the one attached to the IP address. We don't have the names of anyone in the bar that night. We're just starting to investigate. But rest assured, if whoever sent that email is a genuine threat, he will be arrested."

His dad said, "Which is why Ms. Larson won't leave your side."

Axel was just about to agree, when Russ added, "But not as a guard. As your girlfriend."

Axel's brain froze, but Heather out-and-out gaped in confusion. "What?"

Russ said, "Having you pretend to be Axel's girlfriend gives you a reason to be with him twenty-four-seven. At his side. No questions raised."

"Of course, there will be questions!" Axel argued. "For one, everybody knows she's a guard. They'll realize she's a fake."

The King chuckled. "Will they? No one really pays attention to the guards. But just in case, we'll cook up a story about you getting chummy while she guarded you."

Axel held back a wince. Technically, that's exactly what had happened.

Russ glanced at Heather. "The only problem is that in order to date a royal, you would need to resign your post."

At that her face fell. If Axel thought she was

surprised before this, she'd clearly gone to the next level.

Russ winced. "When the charade is over, we'll need to evaluate your position. The press might find the story of you pretending to be the Prince's girlfriend more interesting than if you really had been his girlfriend. If that's the case, then we might decide to hold back the story and make it look like you two just drifted apart."

Heather looked skeptical. "And I go back to guarding him?"

Russ winced again. "You might have to be assigned away from the castle."

"Assigned away?"

"To my parents' home in Paris," the King said. "You'll still have a job. But you might have to wait out some stories in the press before you can return to the castle."

She quietly said, "Okay."

Axel's anger rose at the way his father and Russ downplayed the ramifications of this ruse. She wasn't exactly being demoted but she'd be away from the castle. Away from the action. But worse, she would be the object of scrutiny from the press. The one thing he wanted to avoid, a woman, *any woman he dated*, being scrutinized by the press, was about to become a reality.

He really didn't have a whit of privacy.

Annoyance ground through him, reminding him of the reason he'd gone to that bar that night.

He'd wanted to get away. Instead, he'd thrown himself—and Heather—into the limelight. If they went through with this, it was Heather's life, not his, that would be turned upside down.

"Isn't there another way?"

Russ said, "Another way to what?"

"Keep me protected without involving Heather?"

"You were the one who instituted the policy of having bodyguards act as valets and waiters," his father reminded him. "Hiding guards in plain sight is a very good tactic. Having one pretend to be your girlfriend is an extension of that."

"But the press will tear her apart! Look in every corner of her life. Call the people in her hometown digging for dirt."

"Or we'll clear up the threat in a day or two. She won't be around anymore, and no one will look into anything." Russ sighed. "Don't make more out of this than it needs to be."

The King nodded in agreement. "The two of you go out on the town tonight, so no one is surprised to see her if she has to accompany you to your events." He caught Axel's gaze. "We don't want this guy thinking we're running scared. This has to look real."

"And to that end," Russ said, "we aren't informing the other guards. We don't want to risk a leak."

Axel saw problem number three. As long as this charade was active, her friends might think she was an opportunist, a woman who'd become a guard to rub elbows with the royals, when in reality she'd tried to dodge every attempt he'd made at flirting.

She *had* dodged every attempt at flirting. And once this was over, Castle Admin would issue a press release that said she'd been guarding him not dating him.

Plus, after this meeting he'd get all of Russ's intel and look into this problem himself. He'd go along with his father and Russ's plan. He and Heather would have a date tonight to set the charade in motion and she'd stay overnight in his apartment to make sure nothing happened. But he'd oversee the search for the perpetrator. Probably, this would all be over tomorrow morning.

His father dismissed them, and Axel headed straight for his office. He couldn't believe he'd need more than one day to locate the email writer and decide if they should arrest him or just watch him.

He frowned, running the situation through his brain again. He and Heather would have *one day* when they'd have a date then she'd stay overnight? He almost laughed.

Maybe this could be fun, not the end of the world for her? Especially if he got her out of the limelight before anyone had time to investigate her.

# CHAPTER FIVE

TWENTY MINUTES LATER, Heather left Russ's office. After the meeting with the King, he had walked her to his workspace and emotionlessly given her the barebones rules and requirements of the assignment. He wanted her at Axel's side, twenty-four-seven. That meant she'd be sleeping in one of the bedrooms in his apartment. There would be guards outside the door, but she was the one who would hustle him to safety if someone got on the grounds. Though he doubted anyone would, he believed it a necessary precaution.

She nodded, again not saying anything because she wasn't sure what to say. To Russ, this was business as usual. But Heather kept seeing herself with Axel twenty-four-seven. He flirted like it was his job and there really was an attraction between them. Something earthy and strong—

She winced. Might as well call it what it was. Something sexual. They came from two different social classes, had two different upbringings, didn't share interests. The only thing bouncing back and forth between them was lust.

There. She'd said it.

As instructed, she climbed the stairs to Axel's quarters. One of her peers opened the door to the Prince's apartment for her without as much as a hello, and another bad thing about this secret assignment appeared. Until this was over, she would be a pariah because everybody she worked with would think she was sleeping with the Prince.

Great. Stuck with a sexy flirt she fancied. Hated by her peers. This assignment was officially the second circle of hell.

As the door closed behind her, her anger fluttered away, and her breath stuttered. Not because she was in the apartment of the flirty Prince, but because it was lovely. She expected the hoity-toity, stuffy furniture of Axel's office. Instead, she found modern décor. French country sofas and chairs littered with comfy throw pillows. The fireplace brick had been painted white. Dark hardwood floors gleamed in the sunlight of a window off to the right. Watercolor paintings decorated walls.

This wasn't merely Axel's quarters. It was his *home*. She could see him, feel him all through the rooms as she walked through them, looking for him so she could shake him silly for sneaking out of the castle that night and getting them into this predicament.

But he was nowhere around. The instruction sheet she got from Russ told her the first bedroom in the corridor on the right was hers. Clothing had been purchased for her—as if she didn't know how to dress for a date with a royal—and she should acclimate herself to the apartment and sort the outfits for the events on page two of the list.

Page *two* of the list.

*Whatever happened to this might only be a one-day assignment?*

Not only did she have to spend twenty-four hours a day with the Prince, but she also had homework. Things to memorize. Protocols to process. Manners that told her what she could and couldn't do.

*Man, she was going to give Axel a piece of her mind when he showed up.*

She entered the big closet of her room and something inside her shifted. Packed with dresses, trousers, bathing suits, tops and shoes, it was like the women's department at an upscale boutique—

Not that she needed this many clothes, but since her husband dumped her, she'd decided being pretty was overrated. He'd kept her on his arm like a prize possession—then cheated on her and made her look like a damned fool. She'd shied away from dressing up because it reminded her too much of being a wimp around Glen. Kow-towing to his every wish and whim. Dressing like a princess and not talking. Just being pretty.

That was her only job.

He must have said it eight million times.

When she was finally free, she'd gone in the other direction. Worn dark suits. Blue jeans. Nice T-shirts and tank tops. Not being the pretty girl on anyone's arm. Letting her personality speak louder than her clothes.

Now here she was, confronted by racks, shelves and drawers of femininity.

Her heart fluttered. It suddenly felt like stifling her love of pretty clothes since her divorce had cost her something. She didn't know what it was, but it probably had something to do with the hole she sometimes felt in her soul.

Maybe she could enjoy this...just the tiniest bit?

No. She couldn't. She had a job to do.

She took a long, hard look at the clothes, then shook her head. Knowing she had to match outfits and events, but not quite ready to do that—since the charade might only last a day or two—she went back to the main room to confront her nemesis.

He didn't show up, though.

While she waited, she made a slow, informa-tion-gathering trip through the apartment, sur-prised at the functional French country kitchen, the butler's pantry with hundreds of glasses and dishes, as if Axel regularly entertained here, and a TV room with a pool table.

It made her think of the pool table in the unsavory bar. She smiled, then scrunched her face to stop the automatic good feelings that sprang up. He might have been having fun and she might have ruined *his* fun, but Axel going out had resulted in a threat that resulted in her living with him.

Still alone a few hours later, she sighed at how a guy she was supposed to stick to like glue had totally avoided her. Getting angrier by the minute, she looked at their schedule for that night and saw that a limo would pick them up in about an hour and a half. Regardless of where he was, she had to get ready now.

She winced. She had to get ready to be photographed. To have a microphone shoved under her nose. To spend time with the royal rebel who had ultimately gotten her exiled to the King's parents' house. To pretend she liked him.

In fairness, twenty-four hours ago she wouldn't have been pretending. But that was before she'd been called into the King's office and told she'd have to pretend to be Axel's girlfriend…and, oh, by the way, when it was over she wouldn't be able to work in the castle until the press's interest in her died down—

Her heart stopped.

*They were going to find Maryanne Montgomery.*

Oh, Lord—

She couldn't think about that. Not now. Right now, she had to get dressed. She had to match things, fix her hair, pick sexy shoes.

When she finally emerged from the bedroom and walked to the front room, Axel stood by a back window, staring out over the castle grounds. He looked so handsome in his dark suit, with his hair tied back at the nape, that her breath stuttered, but she cursed it. The man was a pain in the butt, a guy so involved with himself that he didn't recognize what his misbehaving did to others. Her life would become a zoo after this.

And wherever he'd been that afternoon, he'd put her in a position where it appeared that *she'd* disobeyed the order to stick by his side.

"You look lovely."

His eyes sparked, then shifted into the look that probably made women swoon. The predatory gleam that was so sexual, her blood warmed.

She lifted her chin defiantly. She knew she looked good. Who wouldn't in a royal blue cocktail dress that cost what she made in a month and with her hair floating all around her? But adding his natural attributes to the predatory gleam in his eyes, he could wear burlap and exude sex appeal.

Working to stifle the automatic reaction of her hormones, she stuffed a lipstick into the little evening bag she'd found.

"Where were you today?"

He very pleasantly said, "In my office."

"I was supposed to stick to you like glue."

"I talked to Russ. With two guys in my office, two outside the window and two standing sentry at the door, I'm safe." He smiled at her. "After all, it would look silly if my girlfriend came to work with me."

She grudgingly admitted that to herself but refused to admit it to him. Not when there was so much more to this than the happy, fun way he seemed to be approaching it. Thoughts of reporters going to her hometown, peppering the residents with questions about her, hearing about her divorce and the investigation into Maryanne's death rippled through her. She sucked in a breath, telling herself to calm down and pray the ruse would be over too quickly for the press to become curious about her.

"Don't try to be nice."

"Hey, we both have to be nice. That's our charade." He grinned as he walked over to the apartment door. Before he opened it, he said, "Of course, last night it wouldn't have been a charade."

"If you're referring to the fact that you wanted to kiss me, those days are over. This charade will be all business."

"It can't be all business. We're supposed to look like an item."

He opened the door, and they stepped out into

the hall. He nodded to the two guards, then motioned for her to walk to the spiral staircase. They finished the descent to the main foyer and a guard opened the door for them. Heather refused to speak around the guards. Her life was already in enough disarray. There was no way she'd give her coworkers more fodder for gossip about her than they already had.

They slid into the limo and, noting the glass was up between them and the driver, she faced Axel. "We will look like a couple. In public. The rest of the time, you keep your distance."

He pondered that for a second, then said, "You know, if you look at this the right way, we could consider it an opportunity."

"An opportunity?"

"We like each other, but we both know that our being together is off-limits." He smiled hopefully. "Except now it's not."

"Now it's not? What are you talking about?"

"Us. If you think about it, we've been handed the perfect opportunity to explore our attraction without anyone questioning it. You reminded me last night that there's always someone watching me. Now even if they are, everybody thinks we're dating. Even better, behind the closed doors of my apartment there are no cameras, no other guards."

The shock of what he was hinting at rattled her. Especially since her heart stuttered at the thought of exploring their attraction and the automatic reaction of her hormones was breathless anticipation.

Then she remembered that he was a flirt. He looked at her as an escape of some kind and she *did* have to return to being a normal guard—for his grandparents—so far away from the castle she might as well go back to Louisiana.

If this was the perfect opportunity for anything it was to absolutely ruin her reputation, instead of merely having the press uncover her past.

She gaped at him. "Are you nuts! I already told you that you and I aren't a good idea. I'm not starting something with you."

He said, "Too bad," the disappointment in his voice so obvious she felt like a shrew. But what seemed like a fun opportunity for the wayward Prince would be nothing but trouble for her. No matter how attractive she found him, exploring their attraction would not be worth it.

They arrived at an exclusive restaurant. Exiting the limo, she saw the plainclothes guards casually walking up the street. With an active threat on Axel's life, his detail had been tripled. Guards would be everywhere. Though most people wouldn't know it because they looked like pedestrians and other diners.

Inside the cool restaurant, the maître d' clearly knew him well. "Good evening, Prince Axel."

"Good evening, Stephan."

Stephan paused to give her a warm smile, then said, "Right this way, Your Highness."

As they walked toward the back of the room, where a secluded table sat by a wall of windows, affording them a view of the lights of the boats on the lake, she noticed that no one seemed to pay too much attention to them. Though a person or two glanced at the Prince, no one raced over to fawn all over him.

She suspected these were royalty ilk. They might not have a pedigree, but they probably had money. A few might come up to their table to say hello to him as a friend or peer, but there'd be no fawning fans.

Right before they reached the table, Axel slid his hand across the small of her back. Tingles exploded up her spine. She ground her teeth, then remembered they were supposed to be a couple. This was a romance she supposedly had quit her job for. She had to make it believable.

She forced a smile and thanked Stephan as he seated her. Axel ordered wine and Stephan scurried away, eager to do the Prince's bidding.

Axel glanced out the window, then turned to catch her gaze. "This is one of my favorite restaurants in the world. I've been to Paris, Rome, London, New York City—just about everywhere—but there's nothing like a place where the chef knows what you enjoy, and the patrons don't care if you're royalty."

She forced her smile again. In case anyone in the room was watching, she said, "That's great."

He reached over and caught her hand, the way a lover would. Shivers sprinted to her shoulders and cascaded down her spine. She stiffened.

He leaned in and whispered, "We're a couple, remember?"

She sucked in a breath. "Yes."

"If the charade is making you nervous, just pretend it's last night, when we wanted to touch so much we were breathless from it."

She snorted.

He pulled back. "Okay. In the limo, I thought you were being professional. But something's clearly wrong." He paused to study her face, then said, "And it isn't about *you*. It's about me. I did something that upset you. What did I do to make you so mad?"

She almost lied, then decided it didn't matter what they talked about as long as they were engrossed in conversation. This was as good of a topic as any. "Essentially you made it so the press will look into my life."

He pointed at his chest. "I made it so the press will look into your life? This plan is the brainchild of Russ and my dad."

"But you're the one who snuck out that night."

"Look, I have one rule I live by. I protect the women in my life from being hounded by the press. It's why I don't have relationships. I take someone out once, maybe even spend a weekend with them, but I'm with someone else the next weekend and every girlfriend is forgotten. The press calls me a runaround, but they don't look into the lives of the women I see. I have kept my dates safe for a decade by not hanging out with anyone long enough for the media to care. Plus, Russ is sure this charade won't last more than a day or two. Tomorrow morning, if Russ makes the announcement that you and I weren't dating, you were guarding me—you're safe. The press rarely looks into any of my first dates—because they know it's probably the last."

She took a breath. Of all the explanations for why a guy would be a runaround that one actually made sense. In an odd way, it was also gallant. "You think so?"

"Yes."

"I suppose the guards will stop thinking I'm a gold digger once Russ makes the announcement."

"They'll probably praise you."

"So I should relax?"

"I'm thinking we should have fun." He shook his head. "Honestly? I think Russ was being overprotective when he assigned you to guard me twenty-four-seven." He paused to smile at her. "But because he did, we at least have tonight."

"To?"

He took her hand again. "Have some fun?"

She yanked it away. "Seriously, you think we should—"

"Follow through on our attraction? Yes. We should be glad we're getting a night when no one will be any the wiser what we do behind my closed doors."

Her nerves flared with righteous indignation. The way he set that out felt like an insult. As if he was more interested in fooling the guards that getting time with her. Of course, she had already realized he looked at her as a form of escape.

"First of all, you flirted with me. I kept trying to shut you down."

He had the unmitigated gall to laugh. "Tsk. Tsk. Lying to yourself."

Her righteous indignation exploded into genuine insult. "I am not lying to myself."

He glanced at his watch, as if the argument was of no consequence. "Okay. Then you're denying the obvious. We're attracted to each other. I believe we can't hide it. Truth be told, I think subconsciously Russ picked up on it and that's why we chose you for this assignment. We probably look like we should be dating."

"If we do, it's because you constantly come on to me."

He shook his head with a sigh. "I'm not the one with the sparkling eyes when we talk."

"No. You get big bad wolf eyes."

He snorted. "Big bad wolf eyes?"

"Predatory."

He leaned forward. "Really? That sounds kind of sexy."

She groaned.

He took her hand again. She tugged to get it back, but he held fast. "A gossip columnist just walked in. We're on. Angry with me or not, your job is to pretend you're so smitten you want to take me home and ravage me."

The picture that formed in her brain could have made her shiver. She quickly turned her head a fraction to distract herself, but also to make sure he wasn't lying.

He yanked on her hand to stop her. "Don't look! You're supposed to be so enamored with me you quit your job."

She smiled prettily. "No. I was chosen to be the one exiled to your grandparents' house because you can't keep your predatory eyes to yourself."

"When I go home, I'm looking in the mirror to check that out."

"Be my guest."

"And I would also like to remind you that it takes two to flirt."

A quick retort sprang to her lips, but she stopped it. He was right. It did take two to flirt. When he'd asked why she had to be so beautiful, she'd asked him why he had to be so handsome.

There'd also been something between them when he helped her out of the limo—

Okay. So maybe she couldn't blame him completely.

A tall, thin woman with big blue eyes stopped by their table. Axel stood. The woman batted her eyelashes at him. "Hello, Prince Axel."

A ridiculous wave of jealousy spewed through Heather. She almost choked. He might not have singlehandedly gotten her into this mess, but he bore the brunt of the responsibility. She should sell him to the next woman who wanted him, not get jealous.

"Heather, I'd like you to meet Jennifer Stoker. She's a reporter."

Jen laughed. "More like gossip columnist. But I'm told it's my tidbits that sell papers."

Axel sent Heather a significant look. *Don't blow this.*

Heather sighed inwardly. She could be nice to a reporter—while pretending to be Axel's date—but that also put her on Jennifer's radar. Meaning she had to hope the investigation into the threat would be over in the morning and Russ would announce she had been guarding Axel. Then— as had happened with Axel's dates in the past— there'd be no reason for Jennifer to look into her life.

She took the hand Jennifer extended. "It's a pleasure to meet you. Would you care to join us for a drink?"

Axel's eyes widened. "We don't want to interrupt Jen's plans, sweetie."

She had no idea why he appeared so fearful of this woman when two seconds ago he seemed to be reminding her to be nice to her.

She smiled at Axel. "Why not, Pooky Bear?"

His face contorted at her clumsy term of endearment. But he composed himself. "Obviously someone's waiting for her."

"I'm afraid that's true," Jen said, addressing Axel first, then Heather. "But maybe next week we could all sit down together?"

Heather said, "Sure," at the same time Axel said, "I'm sorry. Our week is booked."

Jen laughed at that. "Right." The sarcastic way she said it seemed to intimate that she knew Axel wouldn't be with Heather next week.

That bolstered Heather's confidence in the idea that no one would care about his one-night stands.

"I'll call your assistant." Jen bussed a kiss across his cheek and backtracked to a table closer to the center of the room.

As he sat, Axel whispered, "You never agree to have cocktails with a gossip columnist."

She considered that. "Because of loose lips from alcohol?"

"Because they're evil. They can and will twist things."

"Oh." She frowned. "I thought she was one of the people we were trying to fool?"

"No. She really is a gossip columnist, not a reporter. She won't be at any of the events you might have to attend with me next week. And nine chances out of ten, she won't tell her peers she saw us."

"To keep the scoop about you dating somebody to herself?"

"Pretty much."

"Then why'd you give me that look like you didn't want me to blow this?"

"I didn't. I was trying to let you know she was dangerous because she's a *gossip* columnist and technically this—" he motioned between the two of them "—is gossip."

She groaned. "Does this mean she might look into me?"

"If I didn't have the reputation I do, she might. But what she'll most likely print is a casual mention that I was out on the town. No mention of your name because she knows you won't be around next week."

She frowned.

He laughed. "You know, if she drinks too much tonight, she might forget she saw us." He grinned. "Want me to send over a bottle of champagne?"

She laughed. The first genuine laugh she'd allowed herself since learning of her soon-to-be imposed exile.

He smiled at her. "There you are. The girl I like."

His words sent a flash of pleasure though her.

Though she wanted to curse it, she liked it. When they were normal like this, she liked *him*.

"What do you say we call a truce for a few hours and just enjoy our dinner. I know it's probably weird to be out with me, but every time we talked when you were guarding me you seemed to be able to forget I was royalty."

"I did."

"Because you have a sassy mouth."

She laughed. She liked her sassy mouth. She kept many a client in line with it.

"Are you telling me to dispense with the sassiness?"

He grinned. "No! That's what makes us *us*."

"There is no *us*. There can't be an *us*."

"Okay. How about this? Just be yourself." He took her hand and brought it to his lips. "And I will be putty in your hands."

She didn't get the urge to snatch her hand away. Instead, she got another flash of the woman she'd been before Glen had humiliated her. She'd been confident, sexual…normal. She didn't evaluate every word a man said. She simply had fun.

For thirty seconds she wished she could do exactly as Axel suggested—see this night as an opportunity. But she knew better. She'd been fodder for the gossip mill in her hometown and fodder for the press after Maryanne Montgomery's death. She'd vowed she'd never do anything that would bring undue attention to her again.

No matter how much she wanted to stop being afraid and be herself—her old self, the woman who loved life and people and who wasn't afraid to try new things—she couldn't be. Especially not with a man who attracted more attention than anyone had a right to.

# CHAPTER SIX

THEY ATE A delicious meal and ventured into a dance club, but only stayed a few minutes because of the noise. The drive home in the limo was quiet, but intimate. She'd done such a great job of pretending to be his girlfriend that Axel wondered if she was pretending, or if she had changed her mind about their being together.

He doubted it. She was a very strong person. Because he liked that about her, he wouldn't push, wouldn't try to change her. No matter how much it spoiled his fun.

Still, in the quiet car, on the starry night, with the moon roof open and damp air from the lake drifting around them, he couldn't stop himself from being at least a little happy—maybe more like content.

He'd had just enough wine to be pleasantly tired and he was with a woman he really liked. Instead of trying to figure out everything, he decided to simply enjoy it.

They arrived at the castle. Leo pulled up to the

private entry. Axel exited and helped Heather out. Intimacy radiated around them, like they'd done this a million times before. And his theory of why Russ had chosen her for this assignment popped into his brain. Whatever was between them, it was inescapable.

They entered the small foyer and instead of walking to the steps, they took an elevator to his floor. A guard opened the door to his apartment for them. She smiled but Jeff Gratton stayed as stiff as a stone.

The reminder that the other guards didn't know this was a charade rippled through Axel, as they stepped into his apartment. The difficulty of the situation for her came into focus for him. No matter what anyone said about this being a ruse, some of her peers would wonder what happened behind closed doors. Which was why she would never let anything happen.

Disappointment billowed through him as she slid her wrap off her shoulders. But he was an adult. He saw the ramifications of this charade on her career. He also knew Jennifer might have been the absolute worst person to run into that night. Except his reputation for not having relationships made the women he dated almost irrelevant.She smiled apologetically. "I guess I'll see you in the morning."

"No nightcap?"

"No." She'd tried to say it firmly, but there

was a whisper of doubt woven into the one simple word.

The very fact that she appeared to be tempted reminded him that their attraction was stronger than she admitted. The scoundrel in him hoped the charade outlasted her discipline. But the honest man in him knew that would give reporters reason to look into her life.

She said, "Good night," but took an unexpected step into the formal seating area. As if her body had a mind of its own.

She didn't want to leave any more than he wanted her to leave. They didn't have to kiss. They could talk. Enjoy each other's company. He couldn't remember the last time he enjoyed anyone's company as much as he enjoyed hers.

"One drink won't take away from your beauty sleep."

"You know I don't think it's a good idea for us to get cozy in private."

He stepped behind the bar. "And you know I disagree."

"Then we should each do what we think is right."

Maybe it was the dichotomy of picturing them getting cozy, then picturing them each doing what they thought was right, but he suddenly saw the flaw in their plan of pretending to be dating one minute and ignoring their feelings the next.

He poured bourbon into a glass and added two

ice cubes before he walked to the sofa and sat. "We're both hoping this is over tomorrow, but if it isn't, I think we have a problem."

"A problem?"

"Intimacy. Think this through. If we don't kiss now, behind closed doors, our first kiss will most likely be in public and a *public* kiss can be very revealing. If we don't do it right, it will alert people to the fact that we aren't accustomed to kissing. And people will start asking questions and our charade will look like the ruse that it is."

He could see in her eyes that what he'd said made sense to her.

He rose, set his drink on a coffee table and walked over to her. "The awkward scenario is bad enough, but what if it isn't awkward? What if it's so hot we embarrass ourselves?"

She laughed. "What?"

"Seriously. If you pretending to be my girlfriend goes on any length of time, we're going to be dealing with pent up frustration."

She just looked at him.

"Really? You don't see that happening? You don't see us getting more and more accustomed to each other, closer and closer emotionally…and wondering what it would be like to kiss?"

She cleared her throat. "Maybe."

"No *maybes* about it. We are attracted. True, we're wrong for each other, but don't you think that will only make us all the more curious? And when we do have to kiss—in public—it might not go the way we want it to."

She took a long, slow breath.

"It's my thinking we should kiss in private and get all the animal stuff out, so we don't start a make-out session we can't stop." He paused, giving himself ten seconds to think this through. Knowing she would scamper off the second the kiss ended made this a terrible idea for his libido, but he knew he was right.

If they didn't kiss privately, get themselves accustomed to kissing, there was a good possibility they would make fools of themselves.

She broke the silence. "All right. I see what you're saying."

"Should we set a time to do it—like tomorrow afternoon?"

A horrified look came to her face. "No! Because now that we've thought about it, it's going to hang over our heads. I don't know about you, but I'll worry—"

He didn't give her or himself any more time to think about it. He caught her upper arms, brought her to him and kissed her.

Heather's lungs froze. Breathing became impossible. Especially when she grabbed his shoulders to get her balance and felt the strength of him. *Him. She was touching him.* Not to get him to safety, but just because she could.

The air came back to her lungs, but that only made her aware of the arousal sprinting through her. His lips were warm and experienced, his body solid against hers. Everything she felt for him, the intimacy they could create without trying, the connection, morphed into a physical need so strong she couldn't stop herself from kissing him back.

Which made him bold. He took the kiss from romantic to passionate with a few strokes of his tongue. This time when her breath stuttered it was from hunger and need. Her hands drifted down his back. His fell to her waist and yanked her closer.

*Oh, God! This was exactly what he'd been worried about!*

Given the chance to kiss, they'd sort of exploded.

Her senses came back to her in a rush of intelligent thinking, and she stopped the kiss, yanking herself back, away from him.

His whiskey soft voice whispered, "I told you."

"Yeah. But I came to my senses."

"See? Now we have nothing to worry about. We know what it's like to kiss. We took it a little further than it needed to go, but all the surprises are out of the way."

She rolled her eyes.

"Now we don't have to worry about embarrassing ourselves."

She sniffed in derision and turned to go, but he stopped her. "For the record, kissing you is perfect."

She shouldn't have been a sucker for such an obvious line but kissing him had been perfect too. The way they fit had been perfect. Something about him called to something in her and, if she were being honest with herself, it seemed a shame to have to ignore it.

Then she thought of her ex. Thought of how she always felt out of place with his family, thought of how he'd told her he'd cheated on her because she wasn't enough.

The warmth of humiliation whispered through her, the way it always did when she thought of Glen, but it didn't get legs. It sort of just hung in the air, suddenly meaningless.

Confusion rumbled around in her brain. The thought of Glen humiliating her always kept her in line but tonight it had fizzled. Probably because Axel wasn't like Glen. He was a good person. He would never humiliate her. In fact, that might have been what the first kiss was really all about—a way of acclimating her. So *she* wouldn't be embarrassed or apprehensive or intimidated to let him kiss her in public.

Could he have actually been protecting her?

He'd said he protected his dates from the press, and she believed him. There was no reason to doubt he was protecting her now.

It was all she could do to get her feet moving and send herself down the hall to her bedroom.

She closed the door, then leaned against it, her eyes drifting shut.

The man could kiss. He was a good person. And she liked him. Everything they discovered about each other only brought them closer, intensifying the rightness between them.

But that couldn't be. It *couldn't*. How could a girl from Louisiana belong with a prince?

She reached for the zipper of her dress, but a thought struck her and pure unadulterated joy froze her in place.

*She'd had a surprise kiss.*

She never believed anyone would get around her defenses…but he had. She was about to talk herself out of the joy of that but decided not to. For once, just once, she would enjoy something without tearing it apart.

Of course, she'd never tell him, and she'd be in tip top form tomorrow. He would not get past her defenses again. But tonight, she'd let herself bask in the glow of something she'd believed would never happen.

Friday morning, Axel lay in bed pondering their situation before he got out and headed to the shower.

All his anger about living in a fishbowl, not having a place, had evaporated in one little kiss.

He wasn't a novice. He knew kissing her would be amazing. He'd also anticipated her explosive reaction. They were dynamite together. They were made to enjoy each other's company and set each other on fire.

They were made for a hot fling.

Under the shower spray, temptation almost overruled common sense. He loved being attracted to her. It was terrible having to admit there were consequences, but as a gentleman he had to be fair.

He put on sweats and a T-shirt and went to the small alcove he sometimes used as an office. A few keystrokes on his laptop brought up the day's news, including a picture of himself and Heather, with a mention in Jennifer's column.

Sitting on the chair in front of the small desk, he groaned. Here were the consequences now.

He skimmed her column and decided it wasn't too bad. Jennifer might have printed the picture, but she only had a few lines about Axel being at his favorite restaurant with a date. She hadn't dug into Heather's life. She probably saw Heather as simply a woman Axel went out with once.

Yet another reason to be glad he orchestrated his love life the way he did. The focus of the article was off Heather and on him.

For now. If he didn't go down to his office this morning and get word that they'd found the person who'd sent the threat, Heather would be with him at events. Even if Jen herself wasn't at those events, she would pick up the scent, realize he and Heather were having more than a one-date dinner and start poking around.

He took a breath. Normally, he didn't do things like this, but Heather needed to be protected until the truth about the charade came out and the world would know she was a bodyguard, not a date.

He picked up his phone and called his brother. "I have a problem."

Liam laughed. "I've heard."

"It's more than having a personal bodyguard because of a death threat."

"What's worse than a death threat?"

"Heather and I went out to be seen last night and we ran into Jennifer Stoker."

Liam sighed. "You know your reputation. She probably won't print anything except that you were out on the town."

"I don't want to take the chance that she gets more interested than that. That's why I need your help."

"*My* help?"

"You're the only one with connections to the corporation that owns the newspaper Jen works for."

"You want me to ask my friend to kill the story?" Liam groaned. "Axel, that's a slippery slope."

"Not if you're honest. Tell him the stakes. I got a death threat. Heather's not my date. She's my bodyguard. Ask him to tell Jen to back off for now. And when the whole thing is settled, promise his paper will get an exclusive."

"As head of Castle Admin, you're telling me I can promise his paper an exclusive?"

"Yes. But the story will focus on the death threat with only a mention of Heather pretending to be my date when she is actually my bodyguard."

"That's not the kind of story Jen writes," Liam quietly noted.

Axel took a quick breath. "I know. It's probably going to get assigned to another reporter. But that's the way it has to be. Read Heather's file and you'll understand why I want her role downplayed."

"You're talking about the Afghanistan incident."

"You already read her file?"

"When I saw she'd been assigned to be your personal bodyguard, masquerading as your girlfriend, I decided to check her credentials. And you're right. She doesn't deserve to have that whole thing ripped open again."

Axel held back a sigh of relief. "Thank you."

Liam laughed. "This is a pretty big favor, so you'll owe me."

Axel winced. "I'll take your place at whatever charity event you don't want to attend."

"Actually, there are three."

"I'll do one," Axel said, then disconnected the call. With the situation with Heather sorted, he started to call the kitchen to have them send up someone to make breakfast, but he changed his mind. It had been smart to have Liam put a hold on anything else Jen might print. And, the few lines she did drop into her column that morning might be innocent, but it wasn't something he wanted Heather to wake up to without a warning.

He picked up his phone and called her. There was no answer. Thinking she was probably in the shower, he left a message. "Don't read the news. Talk to me first."

He waited for her to return his call, but twenty minutes went by with him pacing the front room of his apartment without a call.

He paced some more. Read the article again. Tried her phone again. Nothing.

Given that she was a guard, trained to hear and answer her phone, all kinds of ugly thoughts bombarded him. She could be sick. She could have fallen in the shower and be unconscious—

She was an early riser, trained to hear her phone and twenty minutes had passed since his last call. Something was wrong.

He headed to her suite. Telling himself not to panic, he knocked twice. When she didn't reply, he opened the door and peered into the empty sitting area.

The space was eerily silent. Bad vibes and horrible possibilities flooded his brain as he walked into the hushed room. The stillness gave him the creeps. He strode to her bedroom door and knocked. Again, no answer.

Fear hit him like a punch in the chest. He'd been a prince long enough to know that being royal didn't protect you from trouble. After all, he'd lost his mother to a disease that had sneaked into their lives and stolen her. He had no idea what might have happened to Heather. But he wasn't wasting the time running to the front door to get a guard.

He raced into her room, and she bounced up in bed as if he'd awakened her from a deep sleep. Looking around groggily, she said, "What?"

Then she took a long, life-sustaining breath that seemed to wake her up. Completely. With a horrified look in his direction, she grabbed the covers and yanked them to her chin. "What are you doing in my bedroom?"

Still running on the adrenaline of thinking something had happened to her, he said, "What are you doing still sleeping! Not answering your phone!"

"My phone didn't ring."

"I called you!"

She frowned. "Wonder why I didn't hear?"

He shook his head. "Doesn't matter." Feeling like a fool, he forced his breathing to even out, felt his heart rate returning to normal. "Look, there's an article about us in today's paper. I didn't want you to see it before I had a chance to warn you."

Her face fell. "Is it bad?"

"If you mean, is it stupid, yes. If you mean, did Jen dig into your past. No."

She breathed a sigh of relief.

He breathed a sigh of relief. He had royally scared himself into thinking something had happened to her, and it was hard to come down from the spike of fear.

Needing something to do, he strode to the drapes and opened them, bringing morning sun into her room. "She focused on me. 'Prince Axel was out on the town.' That kind of thing. So let's not dwell. Tell me what you want for breakfast and I'll call to get someone up here to cook. We've got an event we have to attend this morning."

He turned from the window with a smile, but with an unobstructed line of vision of her side, he saw nothing but milky flesh, and stopped dead in his tracks. *She slept naked?*

Obviously having seen the direction of his gaze, she shifted the blanket to cover more of her. "All right. You told me. Now, get out."

Fear became confusion, as if his overworked brain didn't know how to process that. "Fine.

Don't thank me for telling you about the article before you saw it and panicked. And don't thank me for calling Liam and having him kill any other story that might come out since he knows the guy who owns the newspaper. Oh, and don't even consider the fact that I only came in because I thought something had happened to you since you didn't answer your phone or any of my knocks on any of your doors—"

"Okay. Thank you." She yanked the cover a little higher. "But go!"

He left, confusion still muddling his thoughts. But he pictured Heather's sheets and covers sliding against all her perfect skin and swallowed hard. Suddenly, she wasn't a fake girlfriend anymore. She was the woman he was attracted to.

After their kiss the night before, he knew she liked him.

He liked her.

She liked him.

And this morning, he'd seen a little more of her than he probably had a right to see. Then he'd gotten flustered. Now things were weird between them. He'd actually sputtered. If he called staff to come to his apartment and make them breakfast, things would be even more strained. Which would not be good for the charade. Or either of them. They needed a chance to get themselves back to normal.

Meaning, if they wanted breakfast one of them

would have to make it. Most likely him because
he wouldn't insult her by asking her to do it.

Heading to the kitchen, he went on a hunt for
bread for toast. Eggs, he knew, would be in the
refrigerator. Coffee, he made for himself every
morning that he didn't eat breakfast. He could
easily make her a couple of eggs and some toast
to give them time to get beyond the weirdness.

It took a while to find bread hidden in countertop cubbyhole with a sliding door. Easy enough,
though, to pop it in a toaster. He had a one-cup
coffee brewer and would have a nice hot cup sitting on the center island, where she could sit on
a stool while he catered to her and showed her
again that he wasn't a bad guy.

The toast popped as she walked into the
kitchen, wearing yoga pants and a T-shirt, still
looking sore at him.

He handed her a cup of coffee. "Peace offering.
I really did think something was wrong and I really did need to tell you about the article before
you saw it, but my good intentions all fell apart."

"Fell apart?"

"You know, once I'd told you about the article I
should have left." Then he wouldn't have opened
the drapes and turned and seen her entire left
side—technically, that's when things fell apart.

She cast him a sour look. "Is there cream in
this kitchen that looks like it's never been used?"

"In the fridge." He walked to the toaster. "And

the kitchen gets used. Just not every day. If I don't have a breakfast meeting, or breakfast with my family scheduled, a cook comes up to make whatever I want."

He turned from the counter just in time to see her roll her eyes.

"That's just protocol. It doesn't make me spoiled. And to prove that, I'm going to cook your breakfast."

One eyebrow rose. "Really?"

"Yes. I've watched the staff do it a million times. Should be easy."

Her lips curved up into a silly smile. "You would think."

He buttered two pieces of toast, put them on a bread plate and set it on the island space in front of where she'd taken a seat on a stool with her coffee.

"Your toast."

Her silly smile grew. "Thank you."

He strode to the refrigerator, retrieved a carton of eggs and headed to the stove. He set the eggs on the counter and frowned. He'd forgotten to get a pan.

He opened three cabinets without finding the pans before she said, "Most people store their pots and pans in the lower cabinets." She motioned in front of her. "Or in the cabinets of the island."

"Good thinking."

He opened a few of the lower cabinet doors, didn't find any pots or pans and went over to the island, where he found several different-sized frying pans. Deciding to make all their eggs at once, he chose the big one.

He waved the frying pan at her. "Thanks."

She smiled at him over her coffee cup. "You're welcome."

He set the pan on the stove, opened the carton of eggs, chose one and cracked it on the side of the pan the way he'd seen the cook do it a million times. Things got wet and sloppy quickly, so he yanked the egg over the middle of the pan and let it drop inside.

The yolk broke. He turned and smiled at her. "Are scrambled eggs good?"

"Sure."

He broke five more eggs into the pan, then got a wooden spoon to stir them. Most of them had already begun cooking, so the white part was already half cooked. But, oddly, he could barely scrape the eggs off the pan.

"You probably should have added some butter before putting in the eggs."

He peered at her. "That's what keeps them from sticking?"

"Usually."

"Well, these aren't too bad." He scraped under them with a wooden thing he'd found in a drawer.

Something with an edge that could do the job better than a spoon could.

Glancing down at them, he frowned. "Not the best looking."

She burst out laughing. "Have you ever cooked?"

"Toast. Coffee," he admitted with a wince. "Not eggs. But I've watched."

Glancing at the eggs, she said, "These are fine." She got off the stool and found two plates in the first cabinet she opened.

"Is there a knack to that?"

She turned to look at him. "To what?"

"Finding things."

She shrugged. "Most kitchens are set up for convenience. I put my dishes above the dishwasher. Looks like your staff does too."

"Okay. Good to know." He took a breath and sat beside her. For a few seconds he was quiet, but annoyance hit him. "You could have told me about the butter sooner."

"You could have stayed out of my room. Or knocked until I invited you in."

"I told you. When you didn't answer, I panicked." He took a breath, shook his head. "Never mind."

"No. I get it. But there have to be lines drawn." She glanced at the horrible eggs. He looked at them too. Dry. Crusty. He doubted even scavengers would eat them.

She caught his gaze. "You should have listened

when I told you I had five brothers. I might not have yelled, but I got my revenge."

She laughed and, damn it, he struggled with a smile. As she left him alone with the eggs, a different kind of weirdness rumbled through him.

He couldn't believe he'd made such a mess of things, but the thought of her hurt had been intolerable, and he'd rushed in without thinking. Still, he'd made it better by not calling a cook and keeping their disagreement just between them, the failure was trying to make eggs.

He frowned, as the oddest thought struck him. Making those eggs was probably the most nonroyal thing he'd ever done. Instead of acting like a respected diplomat, head of Castle Admin, or a rebel prince out for a good time, he thought like a normal person.

Just a guy.

A normal guy.

Trying to make amends to a woman he'd inadvertently insulted.

A chuckle bubbled up and escaped. She'd harassed him as his guard, tempted him in the moonlight and laughed his attempt to make up for a mistake, and he felt normal?

No. He was happy. The sense that he was alone had disappeared. The feeling that there was no place for him had no meaning. He was himself. When he was with Heather that was all he needed to be—all he wanted to be.

He refused to let the ramifications of that become something more than they needed to be. He already knew he liked her. He already knew he respected her. He wasn't going to take it any further than that.

But he also wasn't going to squash it. For once he was simply going to let himself enjoy something normal.

They attended the military awards ceremony scheduled for that morning. Heather wore a pretty white dress that flowed over her flawless body and allowed him a peek at her legs.

She played the role of his girlfriend like an award-winning actress, smiling at him at all the right times. Sometimes when she looked at him the warmth in her eyes took his breath away. But when they returned to his quarters, she slipped into jeans and a sweater and became all business again.

Except she wasn't overly cautious, afraid of their attraction as she'd been the first day. She also wasn't swooning as she had been after their kiss.

Actually, she was back to being normal too, so comfortable with him that their attraction wouldn't stay hidden. With them relaxed and open with each other it also wouldn't feel out of place.

A million possibilities rolled into his head, but he reminded himself he was a gentleman. He also didn't want to go back to the weird situation on the first day of the charade, when it was hard to talk to her and she was angry with him.

He desperately wanted to keep this peace between them, but he was also a realist. The more comfortable they got with each other, the more normal their attraction would feel, and the greater the possibility they would give in to it.

# CHAPTER SEVEN

AFTER A LATE LUNCH, Axel had other meetings and appointments. Without as much as changing his shirt, he scurried away while Heather was stuck in his apartment.

She glanced around the silent space. Russ clearly hadn't thought out how she'd be alone and bored in Axel's quarters every time he was working in his office.

Or maybe he had. Plenty of guards had been assigned to watch Axel while he worked. There were guards on the grounds, keeping out unwanted guests. She didn't need to be there.

She was simply grumpy because she was bored. Finding an available laptop, she pushed a few keys, and the thing sprang to life. Thinking she could play an online game, she found a way onto the internet.

Unfortunately, Axel had it set up to take a user directly to three news outlets. Two were national but one was for Prosperita's main newspaper. Because it was online, not print, they'd picked up the story of that morning's military ceremony.

With her elbow on the desk, she angled her cheek against her palm. The picture of them that accompanied the article showed them by the podium, smiling at each other.

She sighed. She couldn't be mad that they'd made the papers. After all, their first date had been all about setting up the charade that she was his girlfriend, so she could accompany him to events like this one and no one would be surprised. She was on assignment. And, seriously, for a woman who typically didn't wear dresses, she looked really different. Really good. Really *happy.*

The ceremony had been emotional. Prince Axel had presented stripes for promotions and medals for distinguished service. She'd gotten carried away with pride for the servicemen, maybe because she understood their duty, their commitment, their sacrifice.

But she'd also been proud of Axel. In the limo on the way to the ceremony, he told her he'd instituted this event. He kept an eye on service records and easily found the enlisted men and officers who deserved recognition. Then he presented the promotions and the medals.

It was interesting that he'd even thought of that. She'd believed him to be a fun-loving, rebel prince, but all anybody really had to do was take a cursory glance at the things he'd done as head of Castle Admin, and they'd see he worked a little harder than most, dug a little deeper than most.

He was very good at his job. What others perceived as background didn't go unnoticed by him. How could she not be proud of him?

Being proud of him wasn't really stepping into dangerous territory. He was good at his job. He deserved to be appreciated.

It was her happiness she should be concerned about. She'd not only begun to enjoy the assignment, but now she was also understanding Axel, empathizing with him. He wasn't just an incredibly handsome guy who made her breathless. She was beginning to like him.

He returned to the apartment around four o'clock but went straight to his room. He could be miffed at her for laughing at him when he'd ruined their breakfast, but he'd been himself at the military ceremony. Plus, he didn't seem like the kind to carry a grudge over something stupid.

Twenty minutes later, he came out of his room, carrying a tablet.

"Will you join me in the sitting area?"

Standing by the refrigerator, holding a bottle of iced tea, she nodded. She put the tea on the center island and walked over to the sofa.

She sat.

He sat beside her.

Warning bells sounded from her hormones.

He smelled divine and he seemed to emit some kind of pheromone that called to everything female in her.

She reminded herself that she was on assignment, and she was a professional. Attractions and liking someone couldn't matter. She was here to protect him.

Add to that that she didn't want another difficult relationship and she was protected to the max. Even if duty and responsibility failed her, Prince Axel Sokol was out of her league. Way out. So far out, she'd be an idiot to get involved with him.

"I've decided that what we need is a cohabitation agreement."

Surprise had her raising one eyebrow. "Really?"

"Yes." He hit the screen of his tablet a few times, swiped once and started typing. "Because we don't know how long this charade will last, meaning how long we have to live together, it might be a good idea to set out each of our rights and responsibilities, but also some limitations."

That explained why he'd spent twenty minutes in his suite. He believed she was still upset about him coming into her room and he was trying to make up for it. It was sweet enough to make her heart shimmy. But it also proved he was working as hard as she was to assure their relationship didn't step over the line.

It was pretty smart. "Okay. I get it. Like we'll put in don't go in each other's bedrooms?"

"Unless invited."

Her hormones imagined at least ten scenarios in which she would invite him into her room. She thought of her ex, thought of how difficult life had been being the pretty girl on his arm, and shot them down. "You're not going to be invited."

"You're so sure."

"I'm positive."

"Heather…"

He said her name with such skepticism that her eyes narrowed. "You keep forgetting about the lessons learned because of my lousy ex-husband."

He continued typing. "Actually, you've barely told me about your lousy ex." He glanced up at her. "Was he so bad in bed that he turned you off sex? Because if that's the case I have a cure for that."

She sniffed. "No. He was not so bad in bed that he turned me off sex."

"So you like sex?"

Feeling like she'd inadvertently fallen into a trap, she gaped at him.

"Just trying to get the details in the cohabitation agreement correct. We don't want to have to go back and amend this."

"We don't need to write it at all. We're not going to be together much longer. A day or two at best."

He kept talking as if she hadn't spoken. "Okay.

After a preliminary paragraph stating our names and a few whereas clauses that set out our situation and intention, we're ready for point one—no going into the other's bedroom unless invited."

She shook her head. "You're really keeping in the part about being invited?"

"Yes, otherwise when we eventually give in to our roiling passion, we'll never be able to go into each other's bedroom and we'll be limited to the sofa, that countertop and the floor."

She couldn't help it. She laughed. "You are a weirdo."

"Not in the same way as your ex, I hope. But, remember, the offer's still good about that cure."

With a sigh of feigned disgust, she got up and headed for her bedroom to start dressing for dinner. But halfway there, a laugh bubbled up. Sometimes he was so damned normal. Just a normal guy.

But maybe that was the problem? His royal bloodline notwithstanding, he treated her as an equal.

Which was so different than her ex that there was no comparison to be made. That's why she'd been so confused after he kissed her. Axel and Glen might seem the same because of privilege, but Axel was nothing like her ex.

That evening, they had another dinner out in the world, with cameras flashing and reporters yelling questions with a little more interest than the night before. When they returned home, he brought up the cohabitation agreement again.

He walked to a small table against the wall in the main room, opened a drawer and pulled out one simple sheet of paper. "It's ready for you to sign."

She took it from him, glanced at the obvious whereas clauses and only one point. "No going into each other's bedrooms unless invited." She peeked at him. "Where is everything else?"

"You left the room, so I thought there was just one thing you wanted." He peered at her. "Is there anything else?"

Feeling a little foolish, she handed the agreement back to him. "No. Unless I get you to promise not to cook."

"Actually, I thought about adding that one. But trying new things is how one learns. I might need that skill someday so I should practice."

"On me?"

"Why not?"

"Because we've only got another day or two together."

"That's potentially six meals." He paused. "Actually, that's not true. We have breakfast with my parents on Sunday morning."

Her stomach fell. She'd guarded them, spent a week with the King, the Queen and their twins. But going to breakfast? His family knew she wasn't really Axel's love interest. She was guard-

ing him. But that only made it all the more awkward. If they weren't pretending to like each
other—how would they behave?

She suddenly understood the private kiss.
Sometimes they were so attracted—so attuned—
to each other they did really seem to be romantically interested in each other.

She was going to have to really watch her step.

"It's a regularly scheduled weekly thing. Besides, I hear nothing from my family but how
they love you. If we miss the breakfast, they'll
think you don't want to be with them. Worse, they
could think we're down here taking advantage of
the pretend relationship."

"If I remember correctly that was your plan."

"Hey, it's not easy for a man to look smitten
without some...you know, encouragement."

She burst out laughing. "I think we both looked
a little smitten in that picture that was with the
article this morning."

His face turned serious. "Yeah. We did."

The room grew silent. His pheromones reached
out to her hormones and for thirty seconds she
let her guard down, let herself see the real Prince
Axel with his gorgeous hair and hungry eyes.
Their kiss floated into her thoughts and every
feeling she'd had while his lips were on hers returned full force. There was something powerful
and wonderful between them. If they ever made

love, it would probably be amazing. Dazzling. Filled with passion and emotion.

Now she had to go to a breakfast and pretend she didn't feel that.

Because she would never feel it. At least not all of it. She could guess. She could speculate. But this wonderful feeling would go unfulfilled.

She suddenly understood Axel's side of this issue. She'd never felt all this about a man before, and it seemed wrong not to explore it. Was he correct? Was this charade the perfect setup to investigate or enjoy this feeling?

They might not have forever, but they did have now. In a couple of days, she'd probably be on a plane, going to Paris to become part of his grandparents' detail to minimize her exposure to the press.

He stepped back. "I've signed. You sign and leave it on the counter in the kitchen." He turned away. "I'll see you in the morning."

Disappointment shimmied through her, even though she knew she shouldn't give in to her attraction to him. But she also knew he was a good guy, working to do all the right things, who had just gone to his room every bit as disappointed as she was.

Sunday morning, she walked out of her room and to the main room dressed for breakfast with his family. Axel turned when he heard her approach and her mouth fell open and her heart stuttered when she saw him.

Wearing jeans and a T-shirt that outlined his perfect torso, with his hair loose, he looked so good she couldn't move.

He groaned. "My God, you are gorgeous."

She barely heard his compliment as she was hit by the realization of how out of place her raspberry-colored dress and stilettos were. Thank goodness she hadn't put on the fascinator.

"But you're overdressed."

She winced. "Yeah." She winced again. "It's just that I've never had breakfast with a royal family before—"

"You guarded them. Liam too. Just relax. Go put on jeans and a T-shirt. And hurry. Rowan likes punctuality."

She knew that, of course. She raced into the bedroom and found jeans and a top.

When she returned to the main room, he smiled. "Those jeans make your butt look cute."

Knowing he was teasing, she said, "Shut up."

He laughed. "Tell me that upstairs and you will win Liam's loyalty for life."

"I'm not surprised. You mentioned that you tormented him through your childhood."

He opened the door for her. "His fault. He was an easy mark."

When they entered the open area outside his apartment, they stopped talking. Two guards greeted him and grudgingly greeted her. She knew that was only because Axel was there. If she were alone, they would have ignored her, still angry that she'd broken a rule, flirted with a client and was now "dating" him.

They rode the elevator to the penthouse and stepped out onto a main floor. The open floor plan took her gaze to a wall of bifold doors in the back. Beyond them was a huge balcony patio with a view of the ocean, even though it was several miles away.

She whispered, "Wow."

He laughed. "Just relax. Everything will be fine."

"Relax? The ruse is pretending to be your girlfriend. But here, I'm just a bodyguard."

"A cute one," he said, tapping her nose.

"Behave."

He smiled. "See. There she is. The girl I'm smitten with."

"You like me snarky?"

"I just plain like you."

His words had such a ring of truth she believed him—except in his parents' penthouse, they were back to being a prince and his bodyguard. If he got too friendly, things could be more uncomfortable than they were already about to be.

Liam was the first to see them. He set his drink down on the beautifully appointed patio table and raced inside. When he reached them, he caught her hands. "This is so cool. I've never been part of a sting before."

"It's not a sting. It's a charade."

Liam batted his hand. "Doesn't matter. You should be up for an award. You were so convincing at the military event. I watched the clip four times, laughing at how you gazed at him as if you adored him. Hilarious."

Axel gave her a sly look. "Yeah. Hilarious."

Wanting to diffuse Axel's reaction, she laughed. "If I didn't look at least a little smitten, most women would think I was crazy. His hair alone makes most of us swoon."

Axel said, "The sexy hair *is* my thing."

Liam snorted before slapping Axel's back and turning his brother in the direction of the patio. "Everybody's waiting."

She winced.

Axel whispered, "Remember, just be your normal charming self."

"Thought you said I was snarky. Not charming."

"Actually, I think you're sassy. But Rowan will probably like that."

She took a breath. When they stepped out onto the patio, Rowan walked over with two champagne glasses. "Mimosas. It's a tradition."

Axel thanked her. Heather took her glass and smiled. "Thank you."

Rowan impulsively hugged her. "Relax."

Axel put his arm around her shoulders. "Yeah, sweetie, relax."

Rowan gaped at him.

Axel laughed. "Just falling into character to keep my skills sharp."

Heather sighed. As if she wasn't nervous enough, he had to be a jokester. "Stop. Seriously."

Rowan shook her head. "He can be such a pain in the butt. I can imagine he's making your life miserable."

"It's not that bad—" Heather began as the King walked over.

"It's nice to have you here, Heather."

She said, "Thank you, Your Majesty."

Axel said, "I told her no pressure. It's just breakfast."

The King motioned to the open air. "And unless someone has a really long-range lens on their camera, no one can see us."

Sliding her arm beneath Heather's, Rowan led her to the beautiful table. The babbling eighteen-month-old twins were already in highchairs at each side of the King's chair at the head of the table.

The little girl, Georgie, short for Georgetta, had dark hair like her father. The little boy, Arnie, had reddish brown like his mom.

"They're so beautiful."

Rowan grinned appreciatively. "I know. The Sokol genes are great."

Heather said, "That may be true, but I see a lot of you in Arnie."

Rowan laughed. "Yeah. My genes did get a nod. But he's got a devilish side like his father." She led Heather to the seat beside hers, indicating she should sit.

The King pulled out Rowan's chair and Axel got Heather's. He sat beside her, Liam sat across from her and the twins babbled with delight.

"I think they missed you after your week with us," King Jozef said to Heather, opening his napkin and laying it on his lap. He picked up a tray of croissants and handed them to Rowen. She took one and passed them to Heather.

It all seemed so normal—especially with everyone fawning over the twins—that she experienced a wave of something that felt very much like she was living a fairy tale.

When the meal was eaten, Rowan looked at her watch and gasped. "We were having such a great time, I lost track of time." She rose.

Out of respect, everyone quickly got to their feet.

"I'm going to put these two down for a nap."

She pressed a button on her phone and the young man Heather knew was the nanny came out of the penthouse.

"Good morning, Heather."

She smiled. "Nelson."

Before Nelson could lift Georgie out of her

highchair, Axel intercepted him. "Let me help. I've been so busy the past few days I haven't even had a minute with them."

Already holding weepy Arnie, Rowan said, "That'd be great."

Heather watched Axel lift Georgie from her highchair and kiss her forehead. "How are you today, sweet girl?" The baby looked up at him with a beatific smile. He kissed her again. "I missed you guys."

He truly had. Heather could see it in his eyes. He loved the twins and they loved him. She knew he never planned to get married, didn't plan to have kids, and it suddenly struck her as such a shame. He would be a great father.

Rowan said, "We'll be about twenty minutes."

Liam said, "Take your time."

Halfway to the door, Axel turned and gave Liam a look so possessive and primal, Heather's heart stuttered. It was as if he was afraid Liam would steal her away. But they weren't really dating—

Still, they had something.

But it was something they had to ignore. And she hoped she was the only one who'd seen that look.

The King got a phone call and walked to a quiet corner of the patio. Heather and Liam took their seats again.

"They really like you."

She glanced over at Liam. "The twins?"

"The twins, my dad, Rowan." He smiled. "You've made quite an impression on everybody."

She winced. "Not the press I hope."

"Don't worry. That's been handled."

"It has?"

"After your first pretend date, Axel called me and asked me to get in touch with Jen's paper and tell them he'd give them an exclusive after the fact if they pulled back now."

She knew he'd had Liam call the paper and ask them to pull back on the story. She hadn't realized he'd promised an exclusive.

"He did?"

"Look, I read your file. I saw the Maryanne Montgomery tragedy. Like Russ, *I* believed that when the charade was over and we explained you weren't dating, just guarding, Axel, nothing would come of it." He inclined his head. "Axel thinks we're wrong, but even if we aren't he doesn't want to take the chance that they start pawing into your past."

"But won't asking them to back off make them even more curious when we do finally come clean?"

"Maybe. But he plans on giving the interview in such a way that he focuses on his death threat and not your role as bodyguard." He studied his mimosa glass. "He's very good at keeping people safe and seeing what others miss."

"Yeah. He blew me away at the awards ceremony. It might just be my background, but I loved seeing members of the military recognized."

"He sees a lot more than he lets on."

She wondered if that was the thing that had bothered him the night he'd snuck out of the castle and gone to the seedy bar. That the burden of seeing what other people miss finally got to him.

But Liam wasn't the person to discuss that with. Instead, when the silence at the table become obvious, she said, "The twins are certainly adorable."

Liam chuckled. "Our family has changed so much since Rowan joined it. But do you know what? We needed to change. Seeing my father with her and their kids makes me realize everything he was miffed at me for was justifiable."

"Your dad was miffed at you?"

"Oh, please. I'm the Prince who is to become his replacement. He wants me to have an heir."

She laughed.

"I know to an American the idea is probably funny, but we take that seriously here. The papers have printed stories about this a million times. Slow news day...harass Liam about not finding a wife and having an heir." He snorted. "Unless they badger Axel. He took over Castle Admin when it acted more like a maiden aunt who wanted to make sure we wore clean underwear and dated suitable women. He turned it into a necessary arm of royal life. A group that protects us, oversees our diplomatic events…and makes sure we wear clean underwear."

She laughed again. "He sounds like he's found his niche."

"I thought so too until I caught him returning to the castle the night you found him at the bar."

She winced. "I didn't think anyone knew about that."

"I know what secrets to keep." His face filled with concern. "He hadn't snuck out in years."

Because Liam was the one who had brought it up, she carefully said, "He hasn't spoken about it with you?"

"I caught him when he returned and he didn't say anything, except that he was angry with you for catching him. Thought you should be fired."

She laughed. "He does call me sassy."

Liam shook his head. "Really? I rarely see him talk to employees so casually."

"In fairness, I annoy him. I ruined the night at the bar, ruined the run he tried to take my first day on his detail, and now I'm living in his apartment."

"He probably doesn't like having you hover."

She winced. "I have to keep him in line."

"Personally, I'm glad you are. Death threats aren't to be taken lightly." He rose from his seat. "Want another drink?"

She shook her head. "Alcohol and the sun don't mix well for me."

As she spoke, Axel returned. "You're turning down another mimosa, aren't you?"

"I've had two," she said, smiling at him as he sat beside her.

Liam and Axel said, "Lightweight."

They laughed the way siblings do when they have a shared joke. The normalness of it had her glancing around, wondering what she was doing here. She was a commoner, who had a job with a royal family. She wasn't supposed to be eating with them or having private conversations with her client's brother.

A surreal feeling swamped her. She glanced around the beautiful balcony patio again.

She—a smalltown girl from America—knew a king and queen and their children.

She'd dined in beautiful restaurants. Danced at a club she'd normally never get admitted into, ridden in limos, had a whole closet full of clothes—

And kissed a prince who was so handsome it was difficult not to stutter around him.

Axel's voice bought her out of her reverie. "Ready?"

"I'm sorry. What?"

"I was just reminding my family we need to be on our way because I'm introducing the new management at Lilibet this afternoon."

"Lilibet?"

"That's the name of the gallery. The owner named it after his infant daughter. He died unexpectedly last year. Now the torch has been passed."

"Oh."

"We need to dress for that," Axel said, looking at her as if she confused him. She knew why. Normally, she wasn't one for daydreaming. Usually she was on guard. Instead, she'd fallen into the trap of the ruse, amazed to be in this world, feeling like she'd been dropped into a fairy tale. Not doing her job.

She snapped to attention. "I'm sorry! I forgot about that. I suppose we do need to get going."

Liam said, "I'll see you there."

Axel said, "Want to share a limo?"

"No. You're the one making the introductions. You take the limelight. I'll sneak in later. And remember you promised to set up a meeting for me."

They spoke so casually about the gallery and the event that Heather had a little trouble following, but Axel snorted, "I remember." He put his hand at the small of her back and led her to the elevator.

The sense that her life had morphed into a fairy tale returned, getting stronger as they entered Axel's apartment.

The thing that kept rumbling through her thoughts was that this was a once-in-a-lifetime occurrence. Almost like a gift. That's why it confounded her. Things like this didn't happen to average girls from Louisiana—

Except she was here as a guard. Not Axel's real girlfriend. Plus, the charade would be over soon. She could feel it in her bones. She'd checked in with Russ and he'd heard nothing new from the person who'd made the threat. Intel indicated it was business as usual at the bar. Undercover officers reported absolutely no mention of the threat. Every time they'd gone to the bar, they'd seen a bunch of people drinking beer, playing pool. Nothing more. Certainly, no chatter about the threat to the Prince, as if they didn't know about it. It appeared the guy who sent the email had acted alone, and probably impulsively.

As early as tomorrow, they could shut this charade down and send her to Paris.

Becoming part of the King's parents' detail suddenly didn't trouble her because it would be boring. For the first time since this assignment had begun, she realized that when she left the castle she'd never see Axel again.

She tried to tell herself it was for the best, but it didn't feel like it was for the best. She'd miss him. She'd miss his sense of responsibility and his stupid jokes. She'd miss their cohabitation agreement.

But most of all, she'd miss the chance to kiss him again.

# CHAPTER EIGHT

LILIBET WAS A small gallery tucked in a bohemian section of Prosperita's capital city. To Heather's surprise, Lilibet herself wasn't the toddler or little girl she'd pictured when Axel had told her the gallery had been named after her. She'd gone to school in France—where she'd met Axel—and had spent time working at the Metropolitan Museum of Art in Manhattan. A tall, willowy woman with dark hair, and eyes that were more violet than blue, Lilibet Wells was the picture of culture and poise, filled with warmth. And *she* was the person to whom the torch of running the small gallery had been passed.

The event to reopen the gallery was a study in casual glitz and glamor, with well-dressed men and women milling about, sporting diamonds and Rolex watches the way normal people wore department store clothes, generic watches and man-made gems.

But the fun part of the afternoon was when Axel introduced Liam to his old friend. Liam's face lit and Lilibet's eyes filled with pleasure. There was a definitely a spark. The woman Axel had gone to school with seemed like the perfect match for his brother.

The desire to force Liam to take the limo with them when they returned to the castle so she could ask for details nearly overwhelmed her. She had to remind herself that this was a ruse— that she wasn't really friends with Liam—that she needed to stay in her place.

But it was a weak reminder. She'd chatted with Liam that morning like his friend. While she and Axel were admiring a particular painting, Liam had strolled over grinning, making her laugh. Everything felt real. Her connection to Axel. Her connection to Liam, the King, the Queen. She didn't have to fake feelings for Axel or his family. They were real.

As the event neared its ending, Axel called his guards and they left the gallery through a back door, where his limo awaited. His dutiful girlfriend, Heather was at his side with her arm nestled under his.

She put one foot on the pavement and her nerves jumped. Her body stiffened. She glanced around, seeing nothing out of the ordinary, but the air *felt* different. She swore electricity wove around them.

She looked from side to side, again seeing nothing unusual. But what she felt wasn't a physical thing. It was a sixth sense, her bodyguard instincts kicking into high gear.

As if in slow motion, Leo opened the limo door. Axel smiled at her and motioned for her to enter first, but her sixth sense swamped her, and she put her hands on his shoulders, trying to nudge him in first. Then a crack echoed around them. She knew the sound. She'd heard it hundreds of times. Had heard it just before Maryanne Montgomery fell.

She grabbed Axel's arm and all but threw him into the back seat, diving in after him, as another crack exploded through the air.

Axel said, "What the hell?"

"Stay down," she screamed. Guards flooded the alley. "Leo! Get us out of here."

"Yes, ma'am!" He slammed the door closed and jumped into the driver's seat.

She knew at least one royal guard car would follow them, but Leo made short order of the trip to the castle, breaking speed limits, running red lights.

He pulled up to the family's private entry and Heather hustled Axel inside.

In the echoing foyer, he turned to her. "What happened?"

"Someone shot at you."

"Shot at *me*?"

"Well, they sure as hell weren't shooting at me or Leo."

Guards pounded into the entryway.

She pointed to Gerry and Felix. "Take the Prince upstairs. Don't let him out of your sight."

As he was being whisked away, Russ raced into the foyer. "So it's true?"

"That someone shot at Axel? Yes."

Leo said, "You should have seen her. One minute she was normal, the next she got a look on her face and threw Axel into the back seat."

"I heard the crack of the bullet breaking the sound barrier. If the shooter had been a better shot or Axel hadn't moved a fraction of an inch—" She couldn't finish the sentence. The picture that formed in her head almost made her faint.

"Now you see why you were doing what you were doing," Russ said, turning her in the direction of his office. "Come with me."

She glanced back at the stairway, but Russ said, "The others will secure the Prince. Right now, we need an official statement, and we need to figure out what on earth is going on here."

"You don't think it was the guy from the bar?"

He hustled her down the hall, through his secretary's office and into his own, "Emily, get us two bottles of water," he called over his shoulder.

Emily raced in and handed Russ the two bottles before she scrambled out again.

"And close the door," he called after her before he caught Heather's gaze. "The King's going to be here in about thirty seconds. I need to know everything before he gets here."

"We stepped out into the alley, and I got a weird feeling." She looked up at him as he handed her a bottle of water. "I've learned to trust that sixth sense and I was already reaching for Axel when I heard the crack. I shoved him into the limo and told Leo to get us out of there."

"You saved his life."

She shook her head. "Things happened too fast for anyone to think that."

"I said it before. I'll say it again. That's why we had you with him. That instinct of yours."

The back door of Russ's office opened, and King Jozef ran in. "Where is he?"

"In his quarters, Your Majesty," Russ said, rising as the King entered. He glanced at Heather, who had also risen. "I heard Heather giving two guards instructions to take him there and not let him out of their sight, so we'd have a few minutes to debrief."

Motioning for both of them to sit, the King faced Heather. "What happened?"

"We stepped out into the alley. I got a weird feeling. I was turning to hustle Axel into the limo when I heard the first crack. A second crack sounded after we were already inside."

King Jozef turned to Russ. "What's the latest on the bar threat?"

"As you know, the threat was made by an ex-marine with a dishonorable discharge."

"Was he a marksman?"

"Lucky for us…no. But he's been to two different shooting ranges in the past week."

"Arrest him."

"Already on it."

King Jozef turned to Heather again. "You stick with my son. I mean as close as two people can be. Until that shooter's not only in jail, but we're also sure this isn't part of something bigger."

"Yes, Your Majesty."

The King left and Russ said, "You okay?"

"Yeah."

Russ motioned to her water. "Wanna open that and drink it?"

She sniffed a laugh. "Yeah."

"Maybe just sit here a minute until you get your bearings."

"I'm fine. I mean, it's been a while since I've been in this kind of situation, but you'd be amazed at how training comes back to you."

"Training is one thing. Coming down after an event is another. Take some time before you go to Axel's apartment."

She took a long drink of the water, then rose. "No." She needed to see him. She needed to be sure he really was okay.

"His apartment will be surrounded twenty-four-seven. New cameras are being installed on the outside walls in the area of his quarters. Guards in the general grounds will be tripled for the next few days. Until we catch the shooter and we're either sure he acted alone or we've got his coconspirators."

Axel paced the main room of his apartment for about ten minutes before he realized he wanted a shower. He didn't know if it was because it had been a long day or if he needed to wash away the stink of almost being shot, but he headed for his primary suite.

"I'm taking a shower," he told the detail that currently stood by his door and every window in his quarters.

Two guys followed him. They'd already made a sweep of his bedroom, but they went in again, checked his closet, his bathroom and even under the bed before they cleared him to shower.

Dazed, Axel sat on the tufted bench in his closet to remove his shoes. Dizzy and a bit sick in the stomach, he tossed the first one and the feeling was so satisfying, he threw the second one against the wall.

*What the hell had happened?* Oh, he knew someone had shot at him, but his life was normally dull. So dull, he was considering leaving it.

He rose, stripped and walked to the bathroom, where he stepped under water so cold that he shivered.

*Someone had tried to kill him. For going to a stupid bar? Or because they were angry, and Axel made a good scapegoat?*

After a thorough scrubbing, he stepped out of the shower, sniffing a laugh. Not only was he the spare heir, but now he also made a good scapegoat.

Damn, his life was weird.

He dried off. Realizing he hadn't brought a robe in with him, he wrapped a towel around his waist. With everything that had happened, he couldn't be sure there wouldn't be a guard standing in his bedroom, so the towel was a good idea.

He stepped out of the bathroom and saw Heather sitting on his bed. She jumped up when she saw him and raced into his arms. His heart about broke from the jumbled emotions on her face. Fear. Happiness. Confusion. But when she burst into tears his heart did break.

"Hey, I thought big, bad guards didn't cry."

"We don't cry in the moment." She sobbed, peeking up at him. "We wait till our client is safe. Then we find a quiet place to let everything out. Usually, I throw something."

He laughed. Though the situation wasn't at all funny, the release softened muscles that had turned to stone with fear and anger.

That was when he realized she was in his arms, with her arms around his bare back, their bodies as close as two bodies could get with only a towel separating them.

She must have realized it too because she caught his gaze again. Their eyes locked. He bent his head and, nearly as tall as he was, she only had to tilt her face up. Their lips met in a kiss so sweet he could have melted. He hated that he'd been the cause of her worry, her fear.

The kiss deepened as he sought to console her. She cuddled closer. He tightened his arms around her. The kiss ratcheted up another notch as their mouths opened and tongues twined. Then her hands flattened on his back. She grazed her fingers over his skin, raising goose bumps.

The kiss went from emotional to erotic as her hands explored his back. Arousal tumbled through him. Feelings he'd never had with another woman woke like the sun at dawn. His hands roamed her back, along the soft material of the pretty pink dress she'd worn to the gallery reopening. But no matter how smooth and slick the fabric, he knew her skin would be softer.

Everything male in him rose to hot life, insisting that he only had to lift one hand to the top of the zipper of her dress, and he could pull it down and be skimming *her*—not her dress.

The gentleman in him forced him to stop. They'd gone as far as he believed she would perceive to be allowable, and he didn't want to so much as put a nick in her hard-won trust.

He broke the kiss and stepped away, but she pulled him back. He shook his head. "This is about as far as we can go."

She gazed up into his eyes. "I almost lost you today."

The sentiment behind what she'd said hit him right in the heart. He knew she liked him as more than a client. They'd been forming a friendship since she'd caught him at the bar. But the shimmy in her voice and the emotion in her eyes told him so much more. She needed this. She needed to touch and taste and let the joy of life wash over her.

Maybe he did too.

He stepped close. Kissed her again. The tempo slowed. Emotion surrounded them like a comforting summer shower. She kicked off her shoes while they were still kissing. Reached for the zipper of her dress without help from him. It puddled on the floor, and they broke apart so she could step out of it.

Though she'd made all the moves, he still wanted confirmation. He locked their gazes. "You're sure?"

"I'm kind of desperate."

He laughed, reached down and slid his arm behind her knees so he could swing her up, off the floor, and toss her to the bed.

He'd had enough of the fear, the confusion, of knowing someone had tried to kill him. For the next few minutes, he just wanted to be, not think.

He lay on the bed and rolled her onto her back so he could kiss her again. It never occurred to him that there were at least twenty guards in his quarters. Two probably stood right outside his door. With a sitting area separating that door and his bedroom, he decided it didn't matter.

His eager hands touched every inch of her.

For a fleeting moment, Heather thought of the guards too. But her emotions ran too high to care. She'd almost lost him, then he'd kissed her, and all the thoughts she'd been having that day about living inside a fairytale assaulted her. He hadn't died that afternoon, but she was losing him. The investigation had ramped up and those responsible for the note and the shooting would probably be in jail by nightfall. He'd have no more need for a personal bodyguard. And she'd be in Paris. She wouldn't have this kind of access to Axel again. If she didn't love him now, she'd never get the chance.

With one hand on his shoulder, she tipped him onto his back.

He landed on his pillow. "Very funny."

"I'm strong and I don't mind using my powers."

He laughed. The sound was music to her ears and her heart. She pressed a quick kiss to his mouth, then ran her tongue from his chin to his collarbone, down his chest to his washboard abs. "Very nice."

"Your approval makes me glad I go to the gym a few times a week."

"You definitely have my approval."

He let her play, tempt and tease him for only a few minutes before he rolled her to her back and pinned her hands above her head. She knew he'd done it for better access, then his tongue began an exploration of her body and every cell and nerve ending sprang to life. All coherent thought ceased.

He touched every inch of her, caressed until her breathing was shallow and her muscles quivered with need. Then he joined them and for a few seconds the world went silent, still. She'd never thought of sex as being reverent, but there was something about finding the right person—even if it was only temporarily—that stopped her heart and filled her soul.

# CHAPTER NINE

MAKING LOVE WITH Heather had been everything Axel expected and more. She wasn't a shy wallflower. She was herself. Sometimes bold. Sometimes sweet. But very much herself.

Axel lay beside her, his head on his very ordinary pillow, marveling at how his world had turned upside down in a few hours. He'd been shot at. The woman he was closer to than any other person had saved him. Then she'd come to his room and confirmed for him that he wasn't crazy. There really was something between them. Something raw and emotional, but also rare and wonderful—

But he'd just been shot at.

She'd had to save him.

That was part of his life.

Rare and wonderful had been necessary, just what they'd both needed in the moment, but it couldn't be forever. He knew that life in general had no guarantees. But *his* life had been riddled with sacrifice. Now he was the object of someone who wanted revenge or to make a political statement or simply to get his name in the history books. He could never permanently have rare and wonderful. It was why he welcomed what he could get when he could get it.

If he didn't take advantage of every precious minute he had with Heather, he'd regret it.

He rolled to his side. "So are we going to take a nap or what?"

She opened her eyes and smiled at him. "Actually, I'm starving."

"I'll call a cook."

She stopped him with a hand on is forearm. "First, I have to think of a graceful way to get out of your bedroom."

"For starters, I'd comb my hair if I were you." He hoisted himself up to sit, looking at all the beautiful yellow locks that floated around her. "Then I have a few tablets and laptops back here." He angled his thumb toward a small alcove that he sometimes used to work. "You could open one of those and carry it out as if we just had a strategy session."

Her smile grew. "You really do know how to think these things through."

"When I was a kid, I could shimmy down a tree and be at a video arcade before Liam even realized I was gone."

Her eyes narrowed. "How old were you when you started sneaking out?"

He thought for a second. "Probably thirteen or fourteen. Truth is, the hardest part of sneaking out wasn't getting out. It was disguising who I was. That was how I learned to change my voice a bit."

He rose and picked up the towel they'd left on the floor. "But sneaking out takes all kinds of pre-planning and organization. For instance, I made sure I was never photographed in casual clothes. Especially blue jeans. That way no one associated me in anything but my school uniform or formal clothes."

"Wow. You really are good."

He leaned down and kissed her. "I'd like that better if it was a testimonial to what we just did."

She sat and stretched up to kiss him again. "You know you're good at that too."

"And you're spectacular." He grinned. "I told you we should have done this sooner." He grabbed her dress from the floor. "Do you want to shower, or put your clothes back on, grab one of my laptops and go fool your peers?"

She lay down on her pillow again. "What I'd really like is to stay this way for hours, maybe eat steak in bed and do this all over again."

He laughed. "I'm okay with that. But it's your reputation that might take a hit."

"I know," she whined.

"So get up and shower with me, then we'll set up a laptop. Maybe I'll walk out of the bedroom with you, talking about a strategic plan for my safety."

She scooted out of bed. "I like a man who knows how to plan."

He laughed and caught her hand, leading her to the shower.

They hadn't needed to make such a detailed charade for her escape from the bedroom. When they finally emerged—her dressed in the pink sheath and him wearing sweats and a big T-shirt—different guards were in the main room. There weren't twelve as there had been. There were two sets of two. Two guards inside by the door. Two guards in the hall outside the door.

He called a cook to make their dinner. He asked the guards if they wanted in on the meal too, but they declined.

That was when Axel realized that the guards might not have been told that Heather wasn't his girlfriend. Meaning, the charade was still in place.

He walked back the hall to Heather's room, where she'd gone to change clothes. He entered but stopped in the sitting room and knocked on the bedroom door. "I think you might have to let me into your bedroom."

"Just come in!"

He opened the door slightly so he could see she'd already changed into jeans and a comfortable shirt. "Is that an invitation?"

She frowned.

"Cohabitation agreement, remember? I don't want to break any rules."

"You are the biggest rule breaker I know. Just come in!"

"Standing out there with the guards, I realized they still think you're my girlfriend. We might need to go to my bedroom office alcove to call Russ for an update and make sure we're all on the same page."

While the cook prepped dinner, they called Russ. He answered on the first ring. "Your Highness. Everything okay?"

"Yes, I'm here with Heather and you're on speaker. We wanted an update on the investigation, but we also realized that the guards in my quarters still think we're dating."

Russ sniffed. "It's good way to keep Heather at your side."

Heather frowned. "You don't have the shooter yet?"

There was a significant pause. "No. We can't find him." Russ sighed. "We've gone to his house, his haunts. He's gone."

"He's hiding," Heather whispered.

"Yes."

Clearly frustrated, Heather said, "I should be a part of the investigation."

Without a second's hesitation, Russ said, "No. Twenty guards saw you together at the gallery this afternoon. At least eight saw you in the room together this evening. For a week they've believed you were dating. Your behavior today reinforced that. It's the perfect cover. So let's keep that going, shall we?"

Axel grinned at her. She rolled her eyes. "No problem, Russ."

"Good. Go eat. I know a cook went up to your apartment thirty minutes ago. Your food's probably ready."

Axel said, "Thanks, Russ."

Sullen Heather tapped the button on his phone to disconnect the call.

"Why are you angry?"

"I should be working right now. I was at the bar. I was in the alley when the guys raced out after you and you lost your hat. Today, I felt the difference in the air, heard the gunshot. There could be something in here," she said, tapping her temple, "that I don't even know that I know that would be triggered by something we found."

He rose from his chair and caught her hand. "Or you could take a break. You were shot at today too. We've been living a lie for a week. Your brain's got to be tired. Give yourself a few days. If Russ and the team still don't have answers, I can get you in on the investigation."

That seemed to mollify her but that night, lying in bed, cuddled together after mind blowing sex, all those words came back to him. She hadn't only nearly lost him. He'd also nearly lost her.

The thought of it made him squeeze his eyes shut and tighten his arms around her.

It was another reason he didn't do permanent. He didn't fall in love. He didn't get too emotionally invested. He'd lost enough already when his mother died. He could not lose another person close to him and the best way to assure that was to never get close to anyone.

Waking in Axel's bed on Monday morning was equal parts romantic and decadent. They rolled into each other's arms and made love slowly before going to the shower and doing it all over again.

The gallery incident dominated the news outlets. All of Axel's appearances had been canceled indefinitely. He went to work in his office downstairs, but this time she went with him. Their cover was that she was helping with the investigation. Even though she wasn't. Russ barely gave her details of what was going on. Extra guards were everywhere. But every day, the security details slimmed. Where six guards had been posted, there were five, then four, then three, then the usual two.

Though Heather knew Russ and his team were working around the clock to find the perpetrator, figure out his motives and get him into custody, within a few days the rest of the castle returned to normal.

For Heather, the fairytale fantasy came creeping back. Especially when the guards were removed from Axel's apartment. A detail stayed outside the door, but there were no guards in his home.

She made him breakfast, wearing only an apron. The next day, he made her toast, wearing shorts— but no shirt. No shoes.

He cut out of work early every day and they made love in the afternoon. After, they'd swim in the castle's huge pool. He arranged for elaborate candlelit dinners in his apartment. With the exception of the weekly breakfasts they had with his family, it felt like they were on their honeymoon.

Thinking that knocked Heather for a loop. They were trapped in a bubble. So she forgave her brain for tripping over itself with fantasies. It was almost impossible to stop it when they were together twenty-four hours a day.

Two weeks later, the King called Heather and Axel to his office. When they arrived, Russ was already there. Jozef motioned for them to take the seats in front of his desk.

As they sat, Axel said, "What's up?"

Jozef said, "We've hit a wall in the investigation."

Disappointment sizzled through Heather. "What kind of wall?"

Russ said, "Our main suspect is nowhere to be found and we have run out of leads. We put a policeman undercover in the bar you visited, who basically discovered our suspect had been in the bar *the night you met him* but hadn't really socialized with the regulars and hadn't come back. The guy who'd hit on Heather was cleared. The regulars were cleared. But the guy with the IP address that sent the email has disappeared. There's no record of him taking a flight off the island and his car hasn't been spotted by highway patrol."

The King nodded. "His evading capture this long means he's gone underground." He laid his forearms on his desk. "And that sort of takes us to the mood in the country. Axel, you can't hide forever."

Axel sat back in his chair. "Thank God! Do you know how boring it is to go nowhere but your office and your quarters?"

Heather might have been insulted by his outburst, but her sixth sense tingled again. "You want him to make a public appearance?"

"It's been over three weeks," Russ reminded her. "You could do something simple like have a casual afternoon at Lilibet."

"Dress down," the King said. "Make it look like you're visiting your friend." He glanced at Heather. "You could make it appear that you and Lilibet are becoming friends too. It will all seem very normal."

"We won't announce it as an official appearance," Russ said. "So there won't be press or even royal watchers. We can issue a statement about it tomorrow. A fluff piece. And anyone at the gallery who saw you will backhandedly confirm it."

Heather frowned. "You're not trying to draw out the suspect, are you?"

Jozef looked horrified. "Absolutely not. I wouldn't risk my son's life like that!"

Russ said, "But we also don't want the shooter to think the castle is running scared."

Jozef added, "And we *do* want the country to return to normal."

Heather sniffed in derision, "Plus, if the suspect thinks we've stopped focusing on him, maybe he'll come out of hiding?"

"He might," the King agreed. "But that's not our goal."

"I have a cabin on the mountain," Heather said, leaning back as she thought things through. She didn't like any part of this idea. She might see Russ's points, but the King's were a little harder to figure out. Every sense she had about the threat, the shooter, the situation itself, all screamed that it was too soon. Especially since all Jozef seemed to want was to reassure their subjects that Axel was fine. "My cabin's secluded enough that I could hide there for as long as I had supplies."

Russ frowned. "What are you saying? Do you

want to go to that cabin? Become even more hidden than you already are?"

"No. I'm saying that when you get out of Prosperita's cities, there are lots of places on this island to hide. If he's got survival skills from the military, he could elude you for years."

"That's actually my point, Heather," the King said. "We won't stop looking for him. But if he's hunkered down somewhere, Axel is safe, and I want the country to feel safe."

She began to understand what the King was saying. But still questioned it because it caused all her senses to tingle.

Axel had no such problem. That afternoon they were scheduled to go to Lilibet, and he wanted to add lunch at an outdoor restaurant.

"Please?"

She shook her head. "Let's see how the casual trip goes before we start making plans that are too big."

He sighed.

"Don't pout. You're the person I'm trying to protect. You should appreciate me."

He kissed her. "Oh, I do."

Laughing, she playfully swatted him. "Let's go."

Leo grinned as they came out of the castle and headed toward the limo. "It's a pleasure to see you out and about again, Prince Axel."

Axel nodded in agreement. Though he could go

on castle grounds any time he wanted, he made a big deal out of breathing in the air. "Thank you, Leo. It's good to see you too."

Heather rolled her eyes. They eased inside the limo and headed toward the heart of town before they cruised to Lilibet.

Axel groaned. "Wow. I never realized how hemmed in I felt."

"You were fine. And if you don't stop making a big deal out of this, I'm going to get insulted."

"I'm not criticizing your company. I'm just saying that when someone knows they aren't allowed out—going out becomes remarkable."

She studied his face as he spoke. With everything he wanted at his fingertips, the ordinary really was extraordinary to him. She wondered if he realized that he loved life more than anyone knew and craved regular things—things the rest of the world took for granted.

For security purposes, Leo drove the limo into the alley beside Lilibet—not the one in the back where the shooting had occurred—and came around to open their door. To give credence to the casual outing, both Axel and Heather wore jeans and lightweight sweaters. The whole thing looked like an unscripted Thursday afternoon.

Lilibet herself opened the side door to admit them. Axel gave her a hug.

The beautiful brunette pulled back and eyed him as if checking for injury. "I was so worried."

He brushed off her concern. "It was no big deal."

But Heather looked around, studying the area. She picked out the plainclothes guards in the crowd and though there were quite a few, she suddenly realized she didn't trust Axel's safety to anyone but herself. Though her sixth sense had yet to make an appearance today, she nonetheless stiffened with fear as they entered the public area of the gallery.

"There aren't many people here this afternoon." Lilibet winced. "Aside from your guards," she added with a laugh. "Browse to your heart's content."

Axel caught Heather's hand. "We will."

Lilibet looked at their clasped hands and smiled her approval. Heather's warning bells went off, but not with fear for Axel's safety, with concern that their charade was becoming real. People close to him would notice—would *know*—there was something real between them.

She thought about their weekly breakfasts with his family, how comfortable everyone was, how no one talked about the attempt on his life or their fear for him. Her breath caught a bit, but she told herself that she was probably making a big deal out of nothing. Rather than worry about the charade, she should be doing her job. Watching Axel. Making sure no one hurt him.

Lilibet's happy voice seeped into her thoughts.

"I have coffee in my office and some pastries, if you get hungry."

Axel took a deep breath. "We're good. I just want an hour or so of complete freedom."

Lilibet motioned to the paintings. "Go. Enjoy."

# CHAPTER TEN

THOUGH THE TRIP went off without a hitch, Russ called them into his office for a debriefing. Heather told Axel she could go alone, but he insisted on going too.

"We've been out. We are fine. I wish they had arrested the shooter, but if the man is in hiding...then I agree that I should get my life back to normal."

"You know I'm not really been happy with this plan."

Something in her voice warned him that she had real concerns, but he laughed at her overprotectiveness.

"You made the point a few times." He brushed a quick kiss over her lips, then realized how natural that had become. If anyone in on the ruse had seen, they would think it nothing but him perpetuating the charade, but lately he had forgotten they weren't a real couple. Behind closed doors they were and now he felt it in public too. It seemed their charade had shifted on itself.

They entered Russ's office and the head of security motioned for them to take a seat.

"I heard everything went well."

"It did," Heather said.

"And we had fun," Axel added.

Russ sniffed a laugh. "I'm glad but I'm more concerned about how people took your appearance."

"The gallery really didn't have that many visitors. Those who were there kept their distance," Heather said. "They would smile and nod in our direction, but everyone seemed to want to give the Prince his privacy."

Russ nodded. "Everybody knows he's been cooped up."

Axel laughed. "We have an extremely considerate population."

Russ looked pleased with himself.

Heather stayed sober. "I feel like we should still be looking for this guy."

Russ came to attention. "Of course, we are. I didn't mean to make it sound like we weren't."

"We've all gotten so comfortable with this charade, with me being at the Prince's side," Heather said. "That I feel like we're letting our guard down."

"We're not," Russ assured her. "I have people everywhere. Searching. Investigating. We will find this guy."

Heather barely looked appeased, and that might

have only been her attempt to let Russ know she trusted him.

Axel frowned. He hated that she worried about him, hated that his life made her vulnerable to the suspicions and fears that had haunted him his whole life. Other women he dated had been protected from that because of the shortness of their time with him. Heather was literally stepping into the fire, if only because their pretend relationship that had become real had lasted weeks.

Russ's phone buzzed and he answered. "Okay. Thanks. I'll be right there."

"Problem?"

"Actually, that was my wife. She wants me home."

Axel laughed. "Go. We're fine."

Russ gathered his things and left the office with Heather and Axel. After a quick goodbye, he headed for the main foyer and Axel and Heather boarded the elevator.

Behind the closed doors, Heather let out a frustrated sigh. "I don't like being out of the loop."

"We're in the loop."

"No. We're not. We're being spoonfed bits and pieces."

Axel peered at her. She was not going to like what he was about to tell her, but he knew it was the fair thing to do. "I've been getting daily briefings."

She gaped at him. "And you haven't shared?"

He winced. "It's on a need-to-know basis."

Her eyes widened even more. "You don't think I need to know?"

"Russ believes you need to be focused on the present moment, looking for trouble, focused on me. Not investigations that aren't panning out."

"I disagree."

Weirdness rattled through him. The part that was in the real relationship wanted to share with her. The Prince, the guy who needed her as a guard, the guy who trusted Russ, didn't. "Yeah, well, he's head of security. It's his call."

"No. You're his boss. It's your call."

"I don't micromanage. It's part of why the departments run so well. My managers know they have control. And the reports I'm getting are minutia." Fighting with the side that loved their relationship and wanted to be honest with her, he shook his head. "Did you want me to tell you how they looked into my friends to make sure someone wasn't playing a prank or angry with me?"

She sighed. "Yes."

"Then I suppose that means you wanted to hear about how they investigated all my old girl-friends."

She smiled. "That might have been interesting."

"Not really. I never dated anyone long enough for them to be a concern. Not only did they easily clear everybody, but Castle Admin is so good that I'll bet none of those women even knew they were being looked into."

The elevator stopped and they got out.

"If you're trying to make me feel like an idiot for wanting to be in on the investigation of the person who tried to kill the person I'm guarding one-on-one, it won't work. This is my job."

They turned the corner and, seeing the guard in front of his door, Heather stopped talking the way she always did around her coworkers, and he respected that, keeping silent too.

But the minute they were behind closed doors, she said, "Your life is my responsibility."

"And I've now told you everything I know."

"You should have told me immediately."

He took a quiet breath. He hadn't been keeping secrets, but part of him knew he should have shared. Not because she was his guard. Because they were close. Holding back details about his life seemed so wrong he almost couldn't fathom that he'd done it.

The truth of that shocked him silly. Having a public facade that no one could crack was how he stayed sane. Now, suddenly, he wanted to tell Heather everything?

"None of it was significant because everyone Russ investigated was cleared."

"That does make me feel a little better."

Relief fluttered through him, but that didn't stop the strange desire he had to tell her everything about his life, to be really open and honest. "Oh, trust me. We dug deep."

"How deep?"

He laughed. Now it was her turn. Here he was feeling odd because he'd been keeping things from her, but she had her secrets too. "Deep enough to check out *your* ex."

Her mouth fell open. "*My* ex?"

"The story we put out after the email threat was that you and I were dating. Some exes can be possessive. At the very least, having an ex-wife dating royalty might set off some guys. There's no proof that the person who sent the email was the person who shot at me. We had to check it out."

Heather stayed stony silent for a few minutes. He couldn't tell if she was angry that they'd investigated her ex or fearful of what they'd turned up. The only thing she'd told him was that her ex was a louse. Was it any wonder Russ determined they needed to look into the man?

Eventually she said, "What did you find?"

"That he was in the US the whole time. And that he's also involved with two women."

Heather grimaced.

Axel almost enjoyed her discomfort. He'd just suffered the torment of the damned for keeping things from her, when she wasn't any more forthcoming that he'd been.

A million questions formed about her marriage. The desire to know everything about her filled him. But he only said, "Russ's bottom line was that your ex is too busy to care about me."

"And that's all the further you dug?"

"Yes. So if you're worried that I went looking for dirt on you or information on you, you can rest easy." But he was more than a little put off. How could he suddenly long to tell her about himself and hear everything about her, when she was clearly working so hard to keep her life a secret. "Hope that doesn't upset you."

"That my ex is dating?" She batted a hand. "Any woman who wants him can have him."

Her answer was so quick and so sure that Axel's anger leveled up a notch. He knew that sometimes people could grow to hate each other after a divorce, but he could sense that there was a story here. And she wouldn't tell him.

"It really doesn't bother you that your ex is dating two women?"

"He's not my problem anymore."

"Interesting. You think of your ex as a problem."

She sighed. "I really don't want to talk about him."

"Which is exactly what confounds me! If I had an ex-spouse or even someone who'd been important to me, I would tell you. It's what lovers do." The way that poured out of his own mouth astounded him. But he wanted to know that the man meant nothing to her. That her past didn't haunt her. That she had no regrets. "Not that we want to vent but everybody tells their dating history...it's part of how dating is done."

"Couldn't you just believe that Glen and I made a mistake getting married and now that we're divorced, I'm relieved?"

He thought about that. He thought about her. She was pragmatic. But she also had the spirit of a lost soul. This man she claimed to care so little about had hurt her. Axel knew that because he was a lost soul too. His mother had died. He couldn't seem to get a handle on who he was or who he should be. They both had that weird vibe of being too alone.

It was no wonder he felt guilty for keeping secrets and suddenly longed to share his past, his secrets. All along they'd been attuned to each other. They'd understood each other. All that was left was to talk about why.

He very cautiously said, "Sometimes it's the people who have something to hide who won't talk about their past."

"Honestly, the worst thing to happen to me was losing Maryanne Montgomery. After that, having Glen dump me felt puny and insignificant."

"He dumped you after you lost someone you were guarding?"

"My ex was the only son of wealthy people who lived in an average small town. In a way, he was like the 'Prince' of our county. Spoiled rich kid who lived to have fun."

Axel winced. No wonder she had such a suspicious mind about him. Her ex was like the person he felt he needed to be to stay sane.

But surely, she knew him better than that by now?

"He had money. His parents employed everyone else's parents, so he had a weird kind of power. I was thrilled that he even noticed me. We dated two years, got engaged and got married. That whole time I was in the Army Reserves. I went away one weekend every month for training and for a week or so in the summer. He never seemed to have a problem with it. Actually, I think he enjoyed the freedom he had those weekends. Then my reserve unit was called for active duty, and suddenly he was not okay with it. He had his parents pull some strings to try to get me out of it."

Axel gasped. "What?"

She laughed. "It didn't work."

"I should hope not. You're the kind of person who keeps the commitments she makes."

"Exactly." She sighed. "He wouldn't call me or take my calls while I was in Afghanistan. Then the rumors began rippling to me about his cheating. One of my brothers heard that he'd said he was glad I was gone and that he was starting over now. Not waiting for a divorce." She gave Axel the side eye. "That earned him a broken nose."

Axel chuckled.

"When Maryanne was shot, he did call. I grabbed the phone, so relieved that he wasn't the creep everyone was telling me he was. But his first words were that he wanted a divorce. At first, I was shellshocked, then the whole picture fell into place for me."

"He was an idiot."

She shot him another sideways glance. "Or was I the idiot? Aside from refusing to get out of my reserve commitment, I did everything he wanted. I became the pretty girl on his arm."

*Well, didn't that make a weird kind of sense?*

"You're not the pretty girl on anybody's arm now… I mean you are pretty. You're beautiful. Stunning. But there is more to you than that."

"You're damned skippy there is!"

He laughed. "Don't get your panties in a bunch. I've always seen it, remember?"

She looked down. "Yeah."

He lifted her chin with his index finger. The feeling of having her tell him her story was astounding. "Yeah. And I like that about you. I love who you are."

He kissed her. The importance of what he'd said flitted through his brain. He did love who she was. Exactly as she was. It infuriated him that she'd had an ex who'd tried to change her.

Protectiveness filled him. Not that she needed someone to save her, but that he would always let her be herself.

They slid down on the sofa together. Their kiss heated, then ignited with need. It was as if she was telling him she appreciated that he was letting her be herself. So he thanked her with a lovemaking session that he hoped told her everything he couldn't say. But everything he was coming to feel for her.

The worry that they were growing too close crept into his thoughts, but he shoved them aside. There was an end to their time together. They might not know the date itself, but the day would come when the charade would no longer be necessary.

He wanted to enjoy this until then—enjoy being close to someone, really close, for the first time in his adult life. But more than that, he wanted her to enjoy her time with him. Be as happy, as content, as she made him.

So that when they parted, neither would have regrets.

Sated, happy, even happy that she'd told him about her ex, Heather took a long breath and opened her eyes. He gazed at her with an intensity that touched her soul and made her insides quiver. Telling him about Glen had brought them closer. Making love had strengthened the feeling.

The deepening closeness seemed like something they should talk about. If this were a normal relationship that would happen naturally. But they weren't in a relationship. They were two attracted people, enjoying the unexpected perks of a charade. Talking about deep, important things wasn't part of their deal.

Except he was the one who had insisted she tell him about her ex—

He'd even said that's what lovers do. As if he saw her more as a lover than a guard.

It was all too much to think about. No matter what they said or how they defined their roles, she couldn't let herself think it was anything more than a charade. She already cared about him more than she should. If she let herself think his asking questions meant he was getting feelings for her too, she'd tumble over the edge and that would only result in heartbreak.

Wanting to get them back to their normal happy-go-lucky selves before she made more out of their conversation than he intended, she said, "Want a cooking lesson?"

Axel's face scrunched with confusion. "What?"

"A cooking lesson. You said you wanted to learn at least the basics, so how about I find my apron and we go to the kitchen."

"If you're hungry I can call—"

She placed a quick kiss on Axel's mouth. "I like the privacy, the intimacy." That was about as close as she could get to admitting she liked *him*. There was too much of himself he held back. He might have insisted she tell him about Glen, but she knew very little about his past, his personal life. While she was falling for him, he might simply be protecting himself by asking about her.

"After all, we don't know how long we have together. So why don't we make the best of the time we have?"

Axel levered himself off the sofa. "I get the feeling we're together until this is over. And if what Russ said is true, that might be a while."

He turned to go to the kitchen, but Heather caught his hand and stopped him. All this time she'd been falling for him, feeling as if she'd been submerged in a fairytale, but he had been forced to live in hiding. He could go to his office—anywhere in the castle—but today had been his first day out in forever. Worse, from here on out, his events would be a logistical nightmare. Any appearance he wanted to make had to be checked, double checked and then checked again for potential problems. For a man accustomed to living life on his terms, she knew it was stifling.

"Does it bother you that the charade might go on for a while?"

He leaned down and kissed her. "I love having you around."

Part of her didn't doubt that. They never fought. They compromised. They liked the same games, the same movies. She knew he didn't have the kind of feelings for her that she had for him, but she really wanted to enjoy the time they had—

wanted *him* to enjoy the time they had. So they'd both take away happy memories.

But, as his primary guard, it was also her responsibility to make sure she understood him enough that she could keep him from doing something foolish.

"You just don't like being cooped up here?"

"I believe that's exactly what I told Russ."

Relief skittered through her. "Okay. I get it."

He turned to leave but sighed and faced her again. "You know what? You were honest with me about your ex. Now I'm feeling like I'm cheating because I'm keeping something from you."

Her relief short lived, she sat up. She'd always sensed there was something troubling him. She prayed his secret wasn't something that might cause him to do something crazy.

"What's the secret?"

"I snuck out the night we met at the bar because I was feeling underappreciated and maybe like it was time to leave Castle Admin."

Her relief returned. This they could handle. But it also filled her with happiness that he'd decided to confide what troubled him.

"Really? You were thinking about leaving Castle Admin?"

He thought for a second. "Part of the problem is that I did such a good job of revamping the department that it seems to run itself. It runs so smoothly, it appears effortless."

"To an outsider, maybe. But those of us who work for you, especially the royal guard, know that's not true."

"Actually, it *is* kind of true. At least from my vantage point. It's not a challenge for me anymore. The thing is... I don't have a lot of choices or alternatives." He snorted. "Except to go back to being the fun-loving Prince, without a care in the world."

She might have laughed with him, except her sixth sense kicked in. This time it wasn't a threat to his life. It was a clear understanding that his discontent was very real, very serious to him. His brother was the one with all the responsibility because he would be King. But Axel needed to feel useful too.

She chose her words carefully. "This is going to sound odd, but that's exactly what I felt when I returned from Afghanistan. Small towns in Louisiana don't have a lot of openings for bodyguards."

"I guess not."

"When I returned after my tour, I felt like a fish out of water...except I was responsible for my own unhappiness. I was the one who'd joined the Army Reserves. I was the one who'd made myself into someone who didn't fit. I wasn't a small-town girl anymore. I had skills I wanted to use."

The last line caused the expression on his face to change. "That's it exactly. Before I took over

Castle Admin I could jet around the world and convince myself it was my job…like PR. Now roaming around the world seems—lazy." He shook his head. "What should have been an easy decision—leaving a job I've outgrown—feels like a cop out."

"Because you like being useful."

"I don't know if I like being useful, but I like knowing that what I do has meaning. Though running Castle Admin did have a purpose in the beginning—it desperately needed to be updated—now it's not a challenge or even something that people notice."

"The older guards noticed. Promoting Russ, they say, was the best thing you did."

"Yeah. He had the background for the job. Better than the snooty old guy who got the job because it was a step up from being head of housekeeping."

She laughed.

"I'm serious. Castle Admin was a joke back then."

"And it's not anymore."

"It's not anymore."

She considered everything he said, then caught his gaze again. "From what you've just told me, you're very good at spotting things that are wrong and organizing. You have useful skills."

His eyes narrowed. "Are you suggesting that a prince try to get a real job?"

She laughed. "No. I know you and your entourage of bodyguards can't just walk into a corporation every day and work."

"What *are* you saying?"

"I'm saying you have friends, connections. You could start a foundation of some sort. Make a mission statement like providing education to underprivileged kids, sign up your friends to fund it and get to work."

He stared at her, clearly not convinced.

"Axel, there are millions of people in the world with big ideas who'd love to have your connections to be able to get things done. I saw you with those kids who'd won the academic awards. I heard the things you said to them, the speech you gave. Education is a cause you believe in."

For a few seconds he said nothing.

Finally, she sighed. "I'm sorry. I have no business telling you what to do."

"Actually, educating underprivileged kids sounds wonderful. Almost too good to be true." He studied her face. "You got all that from a speech I made?"

"You were very passionate about it. Very proud of the kids. I could tell it was something you believed in."

He continued to study her and warmth rose from her chest to her face. Trying to minimize things, she said, "I'm a very good listener. The point is, your position, your prestige, your power make it possible that you could change the world—or at least a small corner of it."

"I could."

He said it with such certainty that she leaned in and kissed him before she rose from the sofa. Walking into the kitchen nude, she made her way to the pantry cabinet, opened it and pulled out the bib apron the cook had left behind. She slid the loop of the top over her head and then tied the apron around her waist.

He walked into the kitchen after her. "Don't just go doing ordinary things after you've nearly made my head explode with ideas."

She laughed. "What do you want me to do?"

He pulled her into his arms. "I feel like we should celebrate. Maybe go on the internet, think through possibilities."

She shook her head. "That's not celebrating! That's starting the job. And that's for *you* to do. I mean, when I returned home to Louisiana and found there was nothing for me, I didn't ask my mom or dad or even my brothers what I should do. I investigated possibilities. Plus, no one had to tell you Castle Admin was in trouble. You saw it yourself and something inside you made you want to fix it."

He laughed and said, "Okay." But he shook his head. "I feel like I've just been handed a Christmas present."

"I only helped you clear your mind. You've

been a prince so long, you think in terms of your country. But you could help so many more people."

"Yes."

She smiled at him, but her thoughts from the sofa after making love returned. They were no longer casual friends, casual lovers. She'd told him about her ex and he'd told her about his discontent. And she knew him well enough to steer him in a direction that was so obvious he didn't see it.

Warmth and contentment rippled through her, along with a feeling that tightened the muscles of her chest. She absolutely refused to call it love. She called it…connection? No, that wasn't it. They'd always had a connection. This went deeper. And it didn't feel like part of a charade. Didn't feel like two friends giving in to an attraction. It was more, and it was real.

The sense that this was *real* rolled through her. They weren't pretending to like each other. They weren't simply sexually attracted. They weren't just friends. Something *real* had sprung up between them. They had shared secrets. They had looked at each other's lives. Made suggestions. They were fitting into nooks and crannies that never seemed to be filled. And that hole in her heart?

She was wearing dresses, involved in the best relationship she'd ever had, living with a man with whom she fit—just as she was. That hole was gone. She'd simply been so happy she hadn't noticed.

It scared her silly. Not because she didn't want it. Because she was leaving. There was a timetable on this relationship. But even if there wasn't, she could not be a royal. *He* could not marry a bodyguard.

*This would end.*

She let those words roll around in her brain. Let strategies for survival form and solidify. She had to keep things light enough that she wasn't hurt, lonely, when it was over. The new intensity she'd felt, the real aspect growing between them, would have to end.

She slid out of his arms and turned to the cabinet again. "What are you hungry for?"

"What do we have?"

After surveying everything in the cupboard, she opened the refrigerator. "Lots. You think the cook only brings everything he or she needs to make your breakfast, lunch and dinner, but I think she's been stocking the cupboards and this fridge." She opened the freezer section. "Of course, if you wanted something like steaks, we should have already thawed them."

He came up behind her and slid his arms around her waist again. "What are you hungry for?"

She fought not to enjoy his warmth or the way he couldn't seem to resist touching her. Not only did she not belong with him permanently, but she'd also presented him with the keys to a whole new career. Once the threat to his life was over, he wouldn't need her around anymore. He probably wouldn't even think of her.

*That* was what she had to remember.

She took a breath. "Given our time constraints I think I'm hungry for something Italian."

He kissed her neck. "I love Italian food."

"Everybody loves Italian food." She frowned. "Except my one brother."

She turned away from him and he took a seat at the kitchen island. "Really?"

"But he did like chicken carbonara."

He laughed. "There's a story there. I'm starting to recognize how the tone of your voice changes when you mention something that has a story."

Glad for the chance to stop thinking about how he wouldn't even notice she was gone when they parted, she faked a laugh and pulled out the skillet. She set it on the stove, then retrieved some chicken from the freezer. After running warm water into a bowl in the sink, she set the chicken inside.

"That's going to take a half hour to thaw, so what do you say we shower and when we come out, I can make dinner?"

"Sounds good to me."

They showered and dressed in sweats and T-shirts. While she cooked, she told him the story of her brother not wanting to go to an Italian restaurant for her birthday. Her mother had told him that he might not like all Italian food, but she would bet he'd love chicken carbonara. They'd wagered five dollars. At the restaurant, he ordered the chicken carbonara and when it arrived, he snickered as if he was about to make an easy five bucks. But he'd loved it so much that he wanted to lick his plate.

Their other brothers never let him forget it.

Axel laughed. "Your brothers sound fun."

"Just picture you and Liam multiplied until you get five."

"Lots of joking around?"

"A lot of pranks and a lot of loyalty."

"Yeah."

The way his voice changed caused her head to tilt. Talking about his brother was the perfect way to keep their conversations away from themselves so they didn't get any closer than they already were.

"You and Liam are pretty tight."

"We went through something traumatic together. Not just the loss of our mother but the scrutiny of the press. It made us both realize how different our lives were. Made us both understand that we couldn't approach things like normal people. It also showed us there were things we couldn't have."

"Such as?"

He shrugged. "A normal vacation. A night where we could go out on the town and get drunk and say stupid things. Maybe dance on the bar."

She hooted with laughter. "Lots of people might call not dancing on a bar top normal."

He sniffed a laugh.

But something about the laugh didn't ring true. "Does it bother you that you missed out on some things because of press scrutiny?"

He pulled in a breath. "That bothered me when I was younger. What haunts me still is the badgering after our mother's death." He paused. "No. It wasn't just after her death. It was the whole process. Our mother was dying. And everywhere we went someone shoved a microphone under our nose and asked how it felt."

"I'm sorry."

"You have nothing to be sorry for."

She thought about her own parents. The mother she adored. She couldn't imagine losing her, let alone losing her so publicly. In fact, her parents were the only two people she'd let in on this charade with Axel. She hadn't wanted them to worry, if word of her resigning her position to date Axel reached the states. She also trusted them not to say a word. Even to her brothers.

"Close to the end," Axel said, breaking the silence in the room with his voice little more than a whisper. "She wanted to go to our private beach. She was painfully thin and always wore some kind of hat to cover her hair loss. She was also weak. So weak my father pushed her in a wheelchair. So that day, she mentioned the beach and my dad thought it was a great idea. He called Liam and me and told us about the trip. Told us we had to be strong for her and to throw a ball or play some kind of game like it was just a normal day."

Her eyes filled with tears at the sadness in his voice and she nodded. He was telling her the most important story of his life, the piece that made all the other pieces fit. As much as she worried it would bring her closer, she couldn't deny him the support he needed.

"Anyway, we take a limo to the beach. My dad lifts her into the wheelchair and pushes it along a wooden walk of sorts until we got to the sand, then he carries her and sets her up in a beach chair on a blanket. Liam and I go out a bit, toward the water, and throw a ball back and forth. I'm not sure how it happened, but somehow we ended up tossing the ball in front of her and then over her, across the her chair. Dad's sitting on a blanket in the sand. My mother in the chair. Liam and I are tossing a ball, basically over her. And we were all laughing."

"Sounds like a nice family day."

His face softened. "It was. It was the best. She was happy. There was a breeze, but the sun was warm, and she kept lifting her face into the rays.

Liam and I were two clowns, tossing the ball, keeping score of a game we'd made up and my dad sat at my mother's side, soaking it all in."

"Making a memory," she whispered.

He tried to smile. "Yeah. Anyway, it was a good day. We went back to the castle and my dad thanked us. I was a kid, so I remember sort of being proud of myself—but that night she died."

"Oh."

"Yeah. And we woke up to the headlines that while our mother was struggling, Liam and I couldn't even give her the time of day. We played ball and even tossed it over her head without regard for her safety."

She gasped. "That's absurd."

"That's how things get twisted. We gave my mother a good day. The last day of her life was spent watching us play, teasing her, laughing with her. And the two reporters who'd gotten pictures from a guy on a boat with a long-range lens on his camera vilified us."

"They couldn't have known your mother would die that night."

"Really? Does that matter? Why was it important to that reporter that Liam and I look like two crappy sons?"

"I don't know."

"That morning, Castle Admin put out a statement that the Queen had died and instead of the press pulling back on their original story about us on the beach, they made a bigger issue of it."

She squeezed her eyes shut.

"It was ridiculous. But it was also painful. Imagine burying your mother while everyone thinks you didn't love her—had no respect for her or her safety."

"You dealt with it."

He snorted. "Yeah. By feeding into the persona they wanted me to have. By protecting the other people in my life."

"Especially Liam."

"Especially Liam."

And the women he dated. Though she wouldn't say that. He'd given her such a wonderful look into his life, and who he was, that her closeness to him multiplied exponentially. She'd never been as close, as honest, with anyone.

"I don't hate the press as much as I see them for what they are," Axel said. "And I see my life for what it is. People are interested, curious, about us. But they don't want our lives to be as boring as theirs. Even better, they like seeing us as somehow undeserving of the lives we have. The more titillating stories make them happier. So I oblige."

All she had to think about was her own life to understand his. She was an ordinary person who'd made two big mistakes: a bad marriage and the loss of a person in a detail she was guarding. If she'd been a celebrity of any kind, those mistakes would have been examined like a bug under a microscope. And though Maryanne Montgomery's death had been overly examined, the speculation had been limited. Exaggeration had been nonexistent. The investigating body stuck with facts and made sure the press did too.

But Axel didn't have that kind of protection.

No one in his family did.

The burden of it crept up on her. Living as he did would be exhausting. He'd had to sort through all of it to find an identity and keep it, if only to preserve his sanity. It was no wonder confusion over leaving Castle Admin confounded him. No wonder, he sometimes felt he needed to sneak away. No wonder he dated the way he did to protect the women he got involved with.

The kitchen became quiet, but he sniffed the air and gasped. "That smells wonderful."

She spun around to give the chicken carbonara a stir. She knew he'd deliberately changed the subject but decided to indulge him, give him a break from thinking about the past. "And I forgot this was supposed to be a cooking lesson."

"I watched every move."

She shook her head, pretending annoyance though she was glad his voice was back to light and teasing. "I've seen how well you picked up cooking eggs by watching your chef. If you ever decide to make this, there are recipes online. I'll bet you can also find a video that you can follow step by step."

"That's for later." He kissed her. "This is for now."

He said it simply, easily, and she continued to indulge him. But she also recognized so many things she hadn't known before his story. By not having a normal relationship, he was protecting her. Liam might have to get married and produce an heir—either of which could blow up in front of the press—but Axel didn't. He did not have to go through the ordeal of having his personal life dissected in the press and if he was careful, discreet, the women in his life didn't either. He had accepted that. And now, he'd discovered something else to occupy him. Done with Castle Admin, he would create an educational foundation. He could go on to a whole new career, a whole new lease on life.

Without her.

She'd led him to that. Because it was what he needed. He didn't need her. A real girlfriend, a fiancée, or a marriage would only expose him to scrutiny and speculation he didn't want. What he needed was a purpose and she'd helped him find one. She couldn't be sad because it would take him away from her. He wasn't hers. Never would be.

# CHAPTER ELEVEN

THE ENTIRE WEEK of Queen Rowan's birthday was celebrated by Prosperita's subjects. Children gave her flowers as she walked into events. The capital city's women's club held a birthday luncheon. The King made a special donation to the library in her name. On Friday night, the royal family would host a ball in her honor.

Heather had never been to a ball. She'd genuinely believed she wouldn't want to. But she loved Rowan. Everyone did. She also included Heather in family functions as if she were part of the family, not part of a charade. It was especially evident when Rowan called her and asked if she wanted help choosing a gown to wear to the ball.

Given that she didn't have any clue what was appropriate, she breathed a sigh of relief. "Yes. Thank you!"

"I'll call Elegance," Rowan said, referring to her favorite boutique. "They can have ten dresses here in an hour."

Heather's eyes widened. "That would be great."

She knew she'd be spending three month's salary on one dress, but she wanted the dress to be special. More than that, she wanted to keep it, to take it with her when the charade was over. It would be an expensive memento, but she had a feeling this ball would be the most wonderful night of her time with Axel—maybe even of her entire life—and she'd decided holding on to the gown would be the way to keep the memories fresh in her heart.

At eleven o'clock that morning, she took the private elevator to the penthouse and Rowan greeted her as she stepped out. Linking arms, she walked Heather into her dressing room—which was as big as Heather's cabin's living room, dining room and kitchen put together.

A rack of gowns sat in front of a velvet bench and three eager clerks stood at the ready.

Rowan led her to the rack. "Any special color you like?"

Wide-eyed, Heather said, "I like them all."

Rowan laughed. "Pace yourself. There will be hundreds of balls in your life here."

Heather gave her a confused look. Rowan knew about the ruse, so her comment didn't make sense, until Heather remembered the clerks didn't know. So the charade was on.

"Let's start with blue," Rowan suggested, pointing to a beautiful lace gown that one of the clerks pulled off the rack.

She tried it on and loved it but didn't quite feel it was right. "I always wear blue. I think I want something different."

Rowen laughed "Okay. How about red?"

Heather tried on a sleek red gown that was gorgeous in its simplicity, but she hemmed and hawed, nitpicking inconsequential things.

Rowan helped her take it off. "Don't settle. The trick here is to keep trying on dresses until you get the sense that you will be the most beautiful woman in the room."

Heather laughed. "You'll have everyone beat, Your Highness."

Rowan grinned. "I try. But every woman there is the most beautiful woman in the room in her own way. I think what we're looking for here is the dress that makes you feel the most *you*."

Heather reached for a romantic white dress sprinkled with tiny pink, yellow and blue flowers.

Rowan said, "Interesting."

But when Heather tried it on, she never felt more feminine. Though the dress appeared formless on the hanger, it flowed over her curves, as if she herself gave it shape. Her heart tweaked.

Rowan walked around her as if inspecting it. "It's perfect."

Heather touched the ruffle that rimmed the neckline, dipping down in the deep *V* to her cleavage. "It's so pretty."

"It's yours." Rowan pulled an inch of extra material at the waist. Speaking to the silent clerk, she said, "Let's do a measurement. Once it's altered, it goes to Prince Axel's apartment."

The clerk nodded eagerly. After the measurements for alterations were taken, Heather slipped out of the dress and into her own clothes with a happy sigh. As Rowan was occupied with an unexpected phone call, Heather took the main clerk aside. "To whom do I make out the check."

The clerk smiled. "The castle is paying for the gown."

"That's a lovely gesture, but I can pay."

The clerk shook her head. "You'll have to talk with Castle Admin."

Rowan returned from her phone call. She helped the clerks gather their things and when they were gone, sighed with contentment of a job well done.

"You look beautiful in that dress."

"Thanks. But they told me Castle Admin takes care of the bill and I'd like to pay for it myself."

"Nonsense."

"No. It's not nonsense. It's—you know—an independence thing."

Rowan laughed. "I get that. Totally. I was in that place myself. It was extremely difficult to get accustomed to having everything provided for me. But you're on assignment. Protecting Axel." She laughed. "Seriously—even if you weren't— gowns aren't where you take your stand. Vacations are. When you go to Paris or Rome or New York it's much easier to push for what you want."

She appeared to be ready to say something else—probably something that would tie taking a stand into Heather's assignment of guarding Axel—when Nelson came into the dressing room, holding both laughing babies.

Rowan reached for Arnie. "Hey, little guy." The chubby redhead grinned at her. She turned to Heather. "Care to join us for lunch?"

She would have loved to. Georgie's giggle could charm the angels and Arnie was a hugger. But she'd already been away from Axel for an hour. He had other guards, but she was his primary. "I can't." She winced. "Though it doesn't look like it, I'm working."

Rowan nodded. "Go. It would have been fun, but we understand."

Friday afternoon, Rowan surprised Heather by having a hairdresser sent to her room. Axel was still working, so she led the man into the original suite she'd been using, rather than Axel's bedroom suite.

He fussed with her hair for ten or so minutes and asked to see her dress before he simply decided to wash it, curl it and let it be as feminine and romantic as the dress. Heather was about to tell him she could do that herself when she re-

membered what Rowan had said. This was not
where she would make her stand.

As he worked, the hairdresser launched into a
long list of items he would want to happen if he
were dating a royal and though Heather flinched
at first, she realized how accustomed to her the
entire country—including everyone in the castle—had become.

She wasn't merely growing used to being here.
The staff and royals were also growing accustomed to her being around.

She felt it even more when Axel kissed her
after she'd come out of the dressing room in his
suite, ready for the ball.

He looked amazing in his tux with his blunt-
cut hair skimming his shoulders. But his smile
could have lit up the room. "You are the most
beautiful woman in the world."

"Rowan says every woman is beautiful in her
own way."

He laughed. "Rowan is extremely kind."

She picked up her small evening bag, led Axel
through the apartment. When he opened the door
for her, she stepped into the hall. "She is. I can
see why she made such an impact on your lives."

After a short walk, they entered the elevator.
Axel hit one of the unmarked buttons. When the
doors closed, he said, "I sometimes wonder what
life would be like without her. Then I tell myself
not to question our good fortune."

"You shouldn't."

"It's why I don't question you…having you around. You're one of the best things to ever happen to me."

It was the best compliment he'd given to her, and he'd given her some wonderful compliments. But this was beyond personal. It was his honest opinion of their relationship.

It filled her with warmth and wonder that carried her through the brief conversation with the King and Queen, who had decided that the entire family should be in the reception line. Not just Rowan and the King.

Axel agreed. "So many things have changed in our lives the past two months that we need everyone to see we're all here and happy."

Liam laughed. "You always put a positive spin on things."

Axel shrugged. "Nothing wrong with a positive spin." He took Heather's elbow and led her to the entryway that would take them to the front of the ballroom, where they formed a reception line.

She should have felt odd or awkward, but instead she fit. The whole experience that could have flummoxed her felt perfectly normal. As the first in line, they greeted the guests, then quickly handed them to Liam, who greeted them and shuffled them to his father and stepmother.

"We're acing this," Axel whispered to her.

"Because we can get them to Liam so quickly?"

"Yes! That's the skill required here. Everybody wants to chit-chat, so we drive them through with the promise of meeting up after dinner."

She laughed and he kissed her as naturally and easily as a man in a long-term relationship would.

Gazing into his dark eyes, the whole room became silent and still. Everything was so natural and easy with him that the sense that this was real filled her again.

Except this time, she didn't argue. With no word on the shooter and not even a casual mention by Russ or Axel or anyone that this charade should end, what had been a job suddenly felt like the rest of her life. No one even mentioned the threat anymore. Axel had plenty of conversations about it with his dad and Russ, but they were private conversations that he considered confidential. A cog in the wheel of his protection detail, she wasn't consulted. She simply did her job every day, and Axel never talked about it.

She suddenly wondered if Axel was the one keeping the charade intact.

What if he had grown so accustomed to it that he wasn't letting it end?

He had the excuse that the shooter was still at large to keep her in her position as his private guard. So no one would be any the wiser that he simply liked having her around.

The warmth of the possibility rustled through her. This was his family, his world, and he kissed her in front of everyone. His family treated her more like family than a bodyguard.

What if she wasn't the only one realizing their situation had gone from being a charade to being real?

They finished the reception line and walked to a main table, where the King and Queen took the center seats. She and Axel were seated on the Queen's left, with Liam on the King's right.

There were toasts and Jozef gave a beautiful speech about how Rowan had brought love into his life again and love into his son's lives. But when he turned to her and Axel, and publicly introduced her as Axel's love interest, perhaps a new member of the royal family, the whole room erupted with applause. Axel took her hand and kissed it and she honest-to-God thought she would faint.

The King and Queen danced the first dance then Axel led her onto the dancefloor. Though she tried to stop the flood of feelings, they hit with such force that she couldn't deny them.

She belonged here. She *belonged* with Axel.

When she thought about it, she realized they'd been drifting to this point for weeks—and now they were here. The charade wasn't a charade anymore.

They danced another two songs with Heather knowing there were stars in her eyes, but Axel had told her she'd had stars in her eyes every time she looked at him. No one would be surprised, so she went with the feeling. Like Cinderella, she let herself enjoy every second.

When the band took a break, she was laughing with Liam and Axel as Lilibet came over to join them. The beautiful brunette with the violet eyes walked up to Liam with a smile.

She curtsied. "Thank you for inviting me, Your Highness."

He caught her hands. "You're welcome, Lilibet. You look beautiful."

She did. She wore a simple violet gown. A sleeveless sheath with a rounded neckline, the dress was so simple it was elegant. It didn't hurt that it was being worn by an absolutely beautiful woman with impeccable manners, a woman so quietly poised she radiated beauty, but also elegance, dignity—nobility.

This was a woman who was meant to be royalty.

And Liam was clearly smitten.

Axel laughed over Liam's reaction to Lilibet, then laughed again when he saw Liam standing with her on the edge of the dancefloor. The guy had been on maybe four dates with her, not enough to take her as a date to their stepmother's birthday party, so certainly not enough to be in love.

But Liam was obviously in love. The papers were going to go nuts the next day.

Heather pulled back in his arms as he whirled them around in a waltz. "What are you laughing about?"

"Liam."

She turned to find Liam and Lilibet in the crowd. Then she laughed. "They are pretty funny."

"I don't know why you're laughing. You looked at me that way too when we first met."

She sniffed. "So *you* say."

"You did," he disagreed as the waltz ended. The evening was winding down. His father and Rowan had had a wonderful time, but they had twins who were fast approaching the terrible twos. Tomorrow might be Saturday, but babies didn't know the difference between a weekday and a weekend.

"We could actually jump ship right now."

She faced him. Her hair cascaded around her. The dress made her look both innocent and like a wild child. He had no idea how much longer their charade would last, but he loved having her around, so he wouldn't think too long or too hard about it.

But right now, she was frowning at him. "You want to leave?"

"Tomorrow might be Saturday, but I need to work for a few hours."

She laughed.

"Plus, I have something to show you."

"You do?"

"Yeah. Let's go."

She glanced around skeptically. "Don't we have to tell somebody?"

"Nope. I'm the rebel Prince, remember?"

Shaking her head, she followed him as he took her hand and led her through the crowd, but when they neared Liam and Lilibet he couldn't resist stopping.

"Hey, nice party, right?"

Liam shook his head. "What I wouldn't give to have you act normally through an entire event."

Heather said, "I was with him at the military ceremony a few weeks ago. I've seen him do it."

Axel laughed. "I just like to torture you."

Lilibet laughed too, but Axel couldn't help noticing that she was extremely different than Heather. She wasn't stiff. But she was dignified. Poised in a way that spoke of boarding schools and an overprotective mother.

Maybe that was why he'd never been attracted to her as anything other than a friend? Small and genteel, she'd always looked a little bit fragile.

He glanced at tall, gorgeous Heather. She had heart and courage. No one pushed her around—not even him.

Was it any wonder his feelings for her were off the charts?

He told his brother goodbye, then directed her to the elevator that took them upstairs. Guards opened the doors for them, and he was buffeted by the reminder that what he had with her was only temporary.

As soon as the door closed behind them, he spun her around and kissed her. The move was reminiscent of their first kiss, but the passion of the current kiss knocked the memory out of his brain. He almost asked if her dress had a zipper, but he suddenly realized he wanted to make love to the beautiful woman in the dress. He wanted to tangle his hands in her hair and compare the soft fabric of her dress to her skin. He wanted to get lost in her.

He broke the kiss and led her to the bedroom, where one little shove landed her on the bed.

She laughed. "You say my eyes sparkle around you, but you've got the predatory big bad wolf look again."

He put one knee on the bed as he undid his tie and tossed it behind him. "Do I?"

She skittered back a bit. "You do. Like you have something on your mind."

He unbuttoned his shirt. "I have lots on my mind."

"What if I'm tired?"

His belt buckle opened. "You're not tired."

She feigned a sigh. "It's been a long night."

He kicked off his trousers, then pounced. "I know. And this is the perfect way to end it."

He kissed along the neckline of her dress, letting his hands slide down her sides, enjoying the rich fabric, but knowing the skin beneath it was even softer. He skimmed his hands over her breasts, down her sides, teasing her with touches that didn't reach her flesh.

He kissed her mouth again, enjoying the second when he could feel her sink into the moment, forget aesthetics, forget reality. Still kissing her, he shifted enough that he could pull her dress above her hips. Her white silk panties disappeared with one quick flick, and then he was inside her. Joining them the way they seemed to have been meant to be joined. He hadn't intended for things to be so quick, but she was right there with him every step of the way. Their explosion of passion roared through him, leaving him weak. So weak, he closed his eyes and let in the thoughts that always seemed to be knocking on his brain.

Especially one.

He was going to miss her. She hadn't merely protected him these past weeks, she'd helped him find his way.

# CHAPTER TWELVE

HEATHER TOOK A giant gasp for air as he rolled to the pillow beside hers. Their love life never ceased to amaze her but some days he outright astounded her. They lay spooned together for about five minutes before he broke the silence.

"I do have something to show you."

She laughed. "That line reminds me of an old come on."

He snorted. "You think of the weirdest things."

She laughed again.

He rolled out of bed and grabbed one of the laptops in the alcove, while she sat up in bed. After hitting a few keys, he pulled a document on the screen.

"What's this?"

"It's my mission statement."

"Oh!" She reached for the laptop. "Let me see."

He let her take the laptop and, still dressed in her gown, she eased up her pillow, using it for back support. She read the one paragraph mission statement, then the two pages of goals to accomplish the mission. When she was done, tears filled her eyes.

"It's wonderful."

"It's not supposed to make you cry! It's supposed to make you proud of me."

"I am proud of you," she whispered, her heart so full of love she almost couldn't take it. But she suddenly thought of Lilibet. Her subtle poise. Her casual elegance and dignity. The feeling of belonging that had been assaulting Heather lately wobbled a bit, as if it were losing strength.

As Axel launched into a discussion of the reactions of the friends he had already approached for donations, she told herself that "a feeling" didn't matter. Even knowing she was only guarding Axel, Rowan seemed to have accepted her for real, the King accepted her, Liam was becoming a friend.

The only detail they hadn't ironed out was for her and Axel to admit it to themselves.

"I had no idea how many of my friends were looking for opportunities like this."

"Tax write-offs?"

He laughed. "Yes. Most of them. But others are equally interested in doing something worthy with their fortunes. I don't think it will even take me two years to raise the funds I'll need."

"That's great."

He kissed her. "That's *you*. Your influence.

Your help. Your suggestions." He kissed her again. "Thank you."

Torn between the realization that he was clearly ready to jump into his new world and the glow of his recognition that she'd helped him reach this point, she wasn't sure what to feel. Was it time to admit things between them had changed? Was she even correct in thinking that?

Deciding all she could do was stay in the moment, she wrapped her arms around his neck and kissed him. "You're welcome."

He enjoyed the kiss then pulled back. "Now. Let's get this dress off."

She laughed before she rolled to the side of the bed, rose and undid the zipper. He didn't give her two minutes to even consider getting a glass of water or teasing him. He caught her waist and brought her back to the bed.

*Their bed.*

The thought flitted through her brain. It warmed her heart, then it confused her. It all seemed so real, but that didn't change the fact that it was rooted in a charade. Until they actually said it wasn't, declared their feelings, or talked about this being real, it was still part of a charade. It was built on the knowledge that they would separate. When the charade was over, their romance would be over too.

Unless they decided it wasn't.

They had to decide. To say the words out loud.

Part of her believed Axel should be the one to bring it up. But the pragmatist in her wasn't afraid to make the first move.

She simply had to be sure it was the right move.

The next day the King and Queen invited them to dinner to share a birthday celebration with the twins.

To Heather's complete surprise, Liam had brought Lilibet. As Axel and Heather stepped off the elevator, they saw the pair entering the sitting room together and heard them being greeted by the King and Queen.

She held back a laugh. "This could be interesting."

Axel agreed. "Oh, you better believe it."

Axel and Heather entered too, and Jozef rose, along with Rowan, to greet them. "We're so glad you could make it on such short notice."

She knew Lilibet wasn't in on the charade, and that's why the King greeted them the way he had.

Axel said, "It's our pleasure," playing his role.

But was he merely playing his part?

Jozef caught Heather's gaze and motioned to the happy couple, who stood by a tufted sofa. "You know Lilibet, of course."

Axel laughed before walking over to hug her. "I'm the one who knew her first. I introduced them."

Nelson brought the twins into the sitting room, giving one to Jozef and one to Rowan.

Jozef jostled the baby playfully. "And now the real birthday celebration begins."

"You'll love watching them eat cake," Axel whispered to Heather, as they headed to the dining room.

She smiled. "Actually, I'm going to love getting a piece of cake myself. Your pantry is stocked but you have no cookies, no donuts, no cake."

Axel gaped at her. "All you have to do is ask and you can have anything you want."

His words whispered through her...

*All you have to do is ask and you can have anything you want.*

She wanted him. Was it really as simple as asking?

They entered the formal dining room with high ceilings, aristocratic wallpaper and a table long enough to seat thirty people.

As Rowan slid Georgie into a highchair, Jozef said, "We're certainly beginning to fill up this table."

Axel pulled out Heather's chair. "Remember how empty it was after Mother died?"

"The room echoed," Liam agreed, helping Lilibet with her chair.

"And now we have Rowan, two babies and two girlfriends," Jozef said. He kissed Rowan's hand before he faced his sons. "If you two would start having kids, we could have this room filled up in no time."

Axel laughed. Heather reminded herself that the King's comment was for Lilibet's benefit, so she laughed too. But she gave Axel a sideways glance. If he really was pretending for Lilibet's benefit, he should have protested the idea of getting married—and having kids. She and Axel weren't pretending to be engaged. He could have—*should have*—said something to his dad, like "let's not rush things."

Instead, he rolled with it.

His words drifted through her brain again. *All you have to do is ask and you can have anything you want.*

As the conversation drifted around the table, Jozef engaged everyone. He asked Axel questions. Drew Liam into a discussion of oil prices. Asked Lilibet about the gallery and who she saw as the up-and-coming artists. Then he asked Heather how she enjoyed the ball.

Again, remembering Lilibet wasn't in on the charade, she played her role. "It was fabulous. I've never seen so many beautiful people and flowers and decorations. And the food was divine."

The King grinned. "I love bringing new people into the fold. Your reactions always remind me of how lucky I am."

She smiled, not quite sure how to react because this time the King behaved like a man who was really was bringing her into the fold. Liam liked her. The Queen treated her like a prospective daughter-in-law, even in private. Either the charade had gone on so long that his family was getting very good at playing their roles or they really were seeing them as a couple.

She and Axel were going to have to have the conversation tonight.

Though the kids went to bed around eight, the King invited his adult children and their guests to play billiards, and everyone adjourned to a game room. Drinking a glass of rich red wine, Heather sat on the arm of Axel's chair. He soaked in the nice, warm family moment. Rowan watched her husband. Lilibet laughed at Liam, who couldn't take the match from his father.

Axel happily accepted when his father challenged him, and though he came close to beating his dad, he lost too.

When Heather asked to be the next to take him on, Jozef snickered. "Sure."

"Don't be too cocky, Dad," Axel chortled. "She will surprise you."

And she did. She beat him soundly. So did the Queen, which made everybody laugh.

Deciding this was a good time to end the night, Axel caught Heather's hand. "I think we're going to head over to my apartment."

Rowan yawned. "Sorry. But toddlers wear people out."

Jozef laughed. "You can say that again."

Even as he spoke, a butler entered carrying his cell phone. "Your Majesty."

Jozef picked it up off the tray. Clearly annoyed at his family time being interrupted, he said, "Yes. What?" into the phone, then his eyes widened, and his annoyed tone shifted to happy disbelief. "Thank you."

He clicked off the call without a goodbye and faced his family. "Axel, you are free. Not only has the shooter been arrested, but he made a full confession. No conspiracy. No terrorists. Just a guy who'd lost it when he saw you at that bar. Russ sees signs of PTSD. He'll be evaluated in the morning."

Axel spun on Heather, scooping her into his arms and hugging her hard.

Rowan exhaled a sigh of relief.

Jozef said, "This calls for a drink!"

"Actually, Dad," Axel said. "This has been a long ordeal for me. I think I need to go home and decompress."

Liam looked from Axel to Heather and laughed. "Decompress? Is that what the kids are calling it these days?"

Liam's snarky comment reminded Axel that he and Heather really weren't dating. Yet, he'd basically told his brother they were going back to his apartment to relax—together.

Worry about their reaction to his slip didn't bother him as much as the realization that the end of the threat meant the end of the charade. He and Heather would part company soon.

His chest froze and his breathing became choppy. He couldn't picture himself in his quarters without her—

He told himself not to get ahead of himself. There were loose ends to be tied up, and even if there weren't, he could probably persuade her to stay an extra few days, maybe even a week, while the dust settled—especially in the press. The story of her working with him undercover would be received much better if it came out after the arrest of the perpetrator was sorted. With the shooter needing to be evaluated that might takes days, even weeks.

Axel endured a round of goodbyes punctuated by hugs, then he and Heather headed to the elevator that would take them to his floor and his apartment.

In the elevator, he turned and kissed her, reveling in the return of his freedom. When they broke apart, he said, "Thank you."

The elevator doors opened. "I did very little."

He snorted. "You shoved me out of the way of a bullet. That's more than a little."

One of the two guards at his apartment door opened it for them.

They walked into the foyer and the door closed behind them. Heather stopped. He understood the strange look on her face. He was a little shellshocked too. Unsure of what to say or what to do.

Heather caught his gaze and quietly said, "It would have killed me if something had happened to you."

He chuckled. "Your career would have survived."

She didn't take even one step into the main room. "I wasn't worried about my career."

He felt like an idiot. Of course, she wasn't worried about her career. She liked him. He liked her. It really would have hurt her if something had happened to him on her watch.

He walked over and caught her hand, leading her into the apartment, understanding why she was so hesitant. A thought struck him and he paused. What if she was ready to go? Technically, she could pack up and leave now. Their charade *was* over. Sure, he wanted to extend it. What if she didn't?

His heart stumbled. But he quickly composed himself. He never did things on anyone's timetable but his own. He could fix this.

"You know, we can take as long as we want to break down the charade. In fact, I think the story of you going undercover to protect me would play better in the press if we held it back for a few weeks."

"That's what you're worried about? How our breakup will look in the press?"

Confused, he rubbed his hand along the back of his neck. "No. I was clumsily trying to let you know that we don't have to separate right now."

"What if we never separated at all?"

Confused, he said, "What?"

"Axel, we really have been together. I know it began as a charade but think of our first time. Emotion drove us to that."

He remembered. Every damned second of it. Especially the way they'd been so desperate. "You're right."

"We haven't just had fun these past few weeks. We've talked about our pasts. I helped you sort out your problem with Castle Admin. I told you about my ex. You told me about your mother."

She was right again.

He thought he knew what she was hinting at, but he absolutely wouldn't touch this argument with a ten-foot pole unless she really went *there*.

"I don't think I have to go at all." She caught his gaze. "But that's your decision…and from your hesitation I get the feeling I might have guessed wrong."

"Guessed wrong?"

She stepped back, pulling her hand away from him. "I thought you were seeing the same things I was. That we really were happy together. But look at you. The thought of me staying has you all but broken out in hives."

He shook his head. "Don't be ridiculous. If

you're talking about extending our relationship, I'm all for it."

Her breath came out in a relieved puff. "Oh."

"We can spend time at that cabin of yours. You can teach me more about cooking."

Heather had the weird feeling they were talking about the same thing, but they also weren't. She took a second, trying to figure out if that was a sign that what she thought was happening wasn't happening at all. Then she tried to decide if simply continuing their relationship the way it was wasn't the right route. Then she realized she was having trouble figuring this out because in perpetuating a charade they'd done everything backward.

There were things they didn't know about each other. There were normal questions they hadn't asked or answered. Things they didn't know that they would have known about each other if they'd started dating like normal people and eased into a relationship.

But they hadn't.

What they felt might be real, but it was based on a lie.

"I think we have a problem."

He caught her hand and twirled her to him. "Actually, I think we should be done talking so we can enjoy this night. I'm free again."

There was something about the way he said

*free* that snagged her attention. Just when he might have bent to kiss her, she said, "You really like your freedom, don't you?"

"You don't like yours?"

She did. But her need to be an independent loner had been tempered since she'd fallen in love with him.

She let herself say it in her head because up to this moment she'd kept pretending the emotions that swirled through her when she was around him were hormones. It was a form of self-protection that enabled her to be with him, even make love with him, without regret.

But everything had changed now that their charade had become unnecessary. If she let them continue down the road they'd been traveling, she'd wake up one day and realize this moment right now had been their moment of truth and she'd been too afraid to face it.

She was never afraid. Being afraid to disappoint Glen was what had gotten her into a bad marriage where she had to pretend to be somebody she wasn't. She'd vowed never to be that woman again.

She stood tall, waited until he looked at her before she said, "I see us as a real couple. I have for the past three weeks."

He smiled. "I see us as a real couple too."

"Not the way I do."

"And you can tell because?"

"Because if you felt what I do, you wouldn't be so flippant. You'd be a little afraid, but you'd be willing to risk the journey."

That seemed to stop him dead in his tracks.

"You know what I'm saying."

He took a breath. "You love me."

"And you love me too. You just won't admit it."

"Heather." He said her name in his patient, tired voice. "You know better than anyone that I have an unusual, difficult life. It was made harder by the death of my mother. I live in a fishbowl. A long time ago, I promised myself that I would never bring another person into this mess."

"But you did bring me in, and the press has already seen me. The day after our first date, when we ran into Jennifer Stoker, the gossip columnist. And she wrote about me the next day."

"Yes. But she also backed off. I called in a favor with Liam, who called in a favor with the paper's owner to have her not delve into your life. Oh, I'm sure she's looked, but the paper's owner promised nothing would be printed until we gave the go ahead. So tomorrow or the next day or whenever we announce the threat to my life and the capture of the shooter—and the fact that we weren't dating but you were guarding me—your life becomes fair game. The hope is that it will be a flash in the news cycle and fritter out. Because we aren't real. You were just a bodyguard."

She knew all that because Liam had told her.

It was the way he'd said *just a bodyguard* that froze her breath, made her feel small and simple.

"People might poke, but it won't be malicious. They'll be looking for kind things to say about the woman who shoved me out of the way of a bullet. If they find the other things, your marriage, or even Maryanne Montgomery, they will be kind because you'll be a hero of a sort. But if we mention that you are now my girlfriend for real, your life will be torn to shreds."

"And you're saying I can't handle it?"

"I'm not saying that. I'm saying you shouldn't have to. I'm saying the only people who should be in this life are the ones who are stuck here."

She studied him for a few seconds, then shook her head. But he caught her hands before she could speak.

"Please, please understand. And don't leave me. Not yet."

She did understand. She especially understood the desperation in his voice because that same desperation filled her heart. He didn't want her to leave, but he couldn't ask her to stay. He saw his world as a horrible, unhappy place. Not a place he'd curse another person into. Not because he was selfish but because he was selfless.

She fully recognized that now. He'd never made promises. Never said he loved her. He probably didn't love her. He wouldn't let himself. He held himself back from anything that could potentially hurt the people he got involved with.

She would have felt like a fool, except she understood his sorrow. He genuinely wouldn't bring another person into his restrictive life.

His kindness broke her heart.

Still, she couldn't simply walk away, hurt him, because he was hurting her. He needed one more night with her and maybe she needed one more night with him. One night where she savored everything. One more night to hold him close, feel like the luckiest woman in the world, before she would slide out of bed, find the few possessions she'd brought with her the day she was assigned to protect him—and go home.

She caught his hand and led him back to the bedroom, where she let him pretend nothing was wrong. Then, when he fell asleep, she took a minute to study his face, smooth the hair from his forehead, run her fingers along his chest.

Tears filled her eyes. All the things she'd imagined when she began to believe she belonged with him in the castle, all the things she'd known she'd be giving up and all the things she'd believed she'd be getting scrolled through her brain. But no matter how she looked at it, she'd believed being loved by him and being allowed to love him made it all worth it.

She would charge the gates of hell for him, but he didn't believe she should have to bear that burden. He'd lost his mom. Lost his sense of self-worth when the press followed his every move, commented on his every emotion. He would do nothing that would put himself in a position where he couldn't control the narrative.

Having to watch a woman he loved go through their scrutiny was too much for him.

She didn't like having to slide out of bed, slip into her clothes and leave his apartment. She didn't like getting into her SUV and driving forty minutes on the dark roads to her cabin. She didn't like knowing she was going to have to leave her new kitchen and bathroom and return to Louisiana because she couldn't be in his world anymore. Even thousands of miles away in Paris, she'd hear about him, his life, and she couldn't handle that. So she'd give up her job, her cabin, the future she'd had planned for herself.

This wasn't the first thing in her life to go haywire. She had experience with failure and loss. At least this time she'd kept her sense of self-worth and dignity. She'd been her real self with Axel. She'd no longer be searching for herself. She knew who she was.

Odd, that pretending to be someone she wasn't had helped her find herself.

# CHAPTER THIRTEEN

THE FIRST THING Axel did when he woke was reach for her. Finding her spot empty didn't surprise him. She could have woken and slid out of bed so she wouldn't disturb him. But realizing the pillow was barely dented had him sitting up.

Not one to jump to conclusions, he got out of bed. He didn't see her in the bathroom or the walk-in closet, so he slipped into a silken robe and headed for the heart of the house. She wasn't in the main room or the kitchen. Or the TV room where the pool cues lay haphazardly across the silent table.

His heart rate sped up, but he refused to acknowledge it. Instead, he walked to the room she'd used when she first arrived, forcing himself to move casually, calmly. But when he found her closet empty of even the few things they hadn't taken to the main suite—the clothes she'd brought with her—he couldn't stop his heart from falling.

He closed his eyes, acknowledging that her moving back to her cabin, returning to the job she loved as a royal guard, was a disappointment but it was not the end of the world.

Actually, it could be fun. Especially if she'd been reassigned to his grandparents in Paris. He shouldn't assume she'd left him for good. Not when he could see them sneaking around, dating for real on the sly, making love in unusual places. Enjoying Paris on her days off.

That bolstered him enough that he took a shower and went to the main dining room, where he found his dad watching the big screen TV across from the dining table.

"What's this?"

"Russ decided to downplay the threat and attempt on your life that resulted in the arrest last night," the King said, pointing to the screen where video of Russ walking to the podium dominated. Heather stood behind him, to his right, looking very professional in her dark suit with her hair in the ponytail. "The individual Russ's team arrested was evaluated and he has some real problems. He needs time and treatment in the hospital, not more trouble."

If his dad believed that so did Axel. He walked to his chair and said, "Agreed." Glancing at the TV again, he watched Russ answering questions.

The first reporter he called on asked, "You mean the Prince wasn't actually dating Heather Larson?"

"No. Saying she quit her job to date him was

the story we put out in order to provide better security in the face of the threat."

He called on another reporter.

"It looked real."

Russ laughed. "Ms. Larson is a trained guard. She knew she had to make the ruse look real. That's all there was to it."

Twenty hands shot up. Russ shook his head. "It was a ruse. It was a way to provide more security to a prince whose life had been threatened. I'm sorry if that bores you but that's all it was. Now, does anyone have any questions that don't pertain to the ruse."

They did. There were many questions about the originator of the threat. Russ had more background information on the individual than was necessary, but those tidbits went a long way to reassure the press and by extension, Axel knew, their subjects.

The press briefing ended. His dad said, "And that's that."

Watching Heather walk off the stage behind Russ, Axel's heart skipped a beat, but he didn't let any emotion show on his face. Particularly since he now knew why she had gotten up so early—

But she hadn't awakened him. Russ hadn't run any of this by him.

"Why didn't Russ talk to me about this?"

King Jozef said, "You were the object of the threat, and therefore biased. He also feels that his making a statement with Heather behind him, looking like a guard, made the whole thing more professional than personal. With you there, it would have gotten personal."

He nodded, watching the network reporter take over with a recap of what Russ had just said as Heather disappeared from the screen. His dad picked up the remote and turned off the television.

As the screen faded to black, a weird sensation came over Axel. As if someone had erased Heather from his life and shot him back to who he was all those weeks ago when he'd gone to the bar for an escape. When he debated leaving Castle Admin—

Except now he had a plan, a mission statement. He'd already begun gathering funding.

He ate breakfast with his father and endured a round of applause when he entered his office. His staff knew about the threats, of course, but they hadn't known the lengths to which the Royal Guard had gone to protect him.

As he passed his assistant's desk, he heard one of the two guards at the door as he said, "She is going to get such a ribbing when she gets back."

The other guard snorted. "She's not coming back."

*Because she'd been assigned to his grandparents' detail—*

They might not know that, but Axel did. She would be out of sight, out of the minds of the reporters. Russ had handled that press conference so well, Axel genuinely believed no one would bother Heather. There'd be no looking into her past. She was safe.

He felt marginally better and sat at his desk prepared to do two things. Start a comprehensive evaluation of the state of Castle Admin for the discussion he'd have with his father when he handed in his resignation and start a to-do list of the things he needed to accomplish to get his education project off the ground.

There was no better way to accept that his life was different than to keep going in the direction of progress, advancement, his new career—his new life.

*Without Heather.*

His heart tweaked again. But he reminded himself that they could still see each other. Everything genuinely had turned out for the best. He was safe but she was also safe. Her life hadn't been dragged through the mud thanks to Liam's call to the owner of Jennifer's newspaper. Now he'd give an exclusive interview that would distance her even further.

Life was exactly as it was supposed to be with her protected and him moving on.

Thanks to Heather.

Because she was a great person, and she was *not* out of his life. In fact, if he were smart, he'd find a position for her in his new venture. Maybe not a job, per se, but a spot on the advisory board he had to create. Then they could see as much of each other as they wanted.

That eased his mind a bit and he forced himself to go to work on the assessment of the state of Castle Admin, which would include a recommendation of whom he believed should replace him.

He worked nonstop until lunch, not letting his mind go in any direction other than analyzing the department he would be leaving.

At lunch he headed for his father's dining room again. The twins were on either side of his dad's chair, with Rowan to their right and Liam to the left.

His dad snorted when he saw him. "Well, my goodness. You're eating with me two times in one day?"

He chuckled as he walked to the highchair beside the King and kissed Arnie's head. After repeating the kiss with Georgie, he pulled out a chair beside Rowan. "My circumstances have changed."

"Yes, they have," Rowan happily agreed. "And thank God."

Liam said, "Where's Heather?"

He shrugged. "Probably flying to the villa in Paris."

The King frowned. "Flying to my parents?"

"Charade's over," he said, reaching for a big bowl filled with salad. "And that was the plan.

She needed to be out of the castle for a few weeks or months until interest in her died down. So she was assigned to the villa. Once everybody gets accustomed to the fact that we weren't dating for real, she'll be back."

Liam snorted. "Weren't dating for real? Your relationship didn't look fake to me."

Axel glanced at Liam. "We had to make it look real until we understood what was going on. For all we knew that guy could have been a member of a terrorist group. I appreciated having her around."

Liam said, "Right."

His dad and Rowan exchanged a look. His dad winced. "I'm going to go with Liam on this one. I saw you two together. You may not want to admit it but there were some feelings there."

There was no fooling his dad. "Behind closed doors there was more."

His dad looked pleased with his admission, but Rowan appeared to be overjoyed. "Surely, you didn't think we didn't realize you two were romantically involved. Your father and I genuinely believed she was it for you."

Axel gaped at Rowan, then his father. "Is that why you looked at each other just now? You wanted me to—*marry* her?"

"We simply thought you'd found a good match," Jozef said diplomatically.

"Well, I don't want a match," Axel said. Anger

juxtaposed with a longing so strong he wished he could punch something. He was reminding himself as much as his father and brother when he said, "Have you forgotten what we went through? What we always put our romantic partners through? You might have to get married to provide a queen—" he looked first at his dad, then at his brother "—but I don't have to put a woman through the torture of being the object of constant scrutiny." He shoved away from the table and strode out, so angry he almost couldn't see straight.

Worse, he couldn't really say why he was angry. He'd lived with this reality for over two decades. Seen the horrible underbelly of the media when he'd lost his mom. Made decisions that had kept him sane and reasonably happy.

He almost headed back to his office but changed his mind, going to his apartment. He ignored the empty feel of it, called for someone from the kitchen and then ate his lunch alone.

When he was done eating, he still didn't feel like going back to his office, so he retrieved one of his laptops, settled himself on the sofa in the main room and went back to work on the evaluation of Castel Admin.

After only a few minutes there was a knock on his door. Rowan said, "Axel? Are you okay?"

Axel groaned. He wanted neither a lecture nor sympathy.

He pulled in a breath, pasted a smile on his face and said, "I'm fine."

"Great, then I'm coming in."

She entered and walked over to him. Before she could say anything about him storming out of the dining room, he took control of the conversation. "I think the stress of having my life in danger for so long and essentially living with somebody is all crashing down on me."

Rowan smiled and took a step closer. "We all sometimes do keep a brave face during a problem, then fall apart when it's over." She laughed lightly. "When we should be celebrating."

Relief billowed through Axel. She seemed to totally understand. "Yeah. I think that's it."

She waited a second then added, "There is one thing that I don't think you've been told."

He caught her gaze. "Something I haven't been told?"

"After lunch, I made some calls. From what you said in the dining room, I don't think you know Heather's gone."

"Gone?"

"She quit this morning. She told Russ she thought it was time for her to go back home to Louisiana. That's all she said."

He tried to work that out in his brain. All morning long, he'd fought the sadness over her loss, thinking she was in Paris. But hearing she was returning to the States punctured his heart.

Rowan said, "Your dad thought the strain of guarding you when you were under a threat might have been too much for her. I don't agree. She was the one who watched you twenty-four-seven. She's the one who shoved you out of the way of a bullet. She was one tough cookie. I never saw a sign of stress on her face."

Axel mumbled, "Neither did I." But he hadn't been looking. For as much as he took the threat seriously, she'd taken such good care of him that he'd never even considered that she'd been working—well, he had. But not the way he should have.

He licked his suddenly dry lips. "You know what? I'm just going to go back to work now." He tried his best smile.

Rowan shook her head. "Axel, for heaven's sake. That woman loves you. It was always written all over her face. And you love her too. Don't throw away something this special."

Axel quietly said, "I promised myself long ago I wouldn't force a woman into this life. Of all people, Heather wouldn't want it."

"Have you asked?"

His gaze shot to Rowan's. "No. Because she doesn't really know what she would be getting herself into. We don't merely have the stress of our lives—we aren't above the laws of nature. And when we lose someone, something, face a problem, make a fool of ourselves, make a mistake, the whole world is watching. I won't go through that again and I won't put a woman through it."

Rowan frowned. "So you've just decided to never get close to anyone?"

"Yes. No." He ran his fingers through his hair. "It's not that simple."

"Isn't it? Out of fear of having your emotions play out for the world to see you'll deprive yourself of love forever?"

"I have plenty of love in my life."

Rowan laughed. "Oh, sweetie. You have plenty of sex. Not love." She paused for a second and studied Axel. "Don't do this. Don't let her get away."

"You say that as if it's my choice."

She caught his arm and squeezed. "It is. And once you see that, your whole world will change."

Axel almost argued but when Rowan walked out of his apartment, he knew the conversation was over. He gathered his things and went to his office, shaking his head. This was not his choice. It was how he had to live to keep his sanity—

Of course, not wanting to be the object of the newspapers' scorn and ridicule—*that* was a choice. Technically, he could let them print what they wanted and ignore it. Or combat it. Have a press conference in which he set the record straight—

No. He had to protect Heather. Whether she

understood it or not, this loss he felt was necessary to protect her.

But that night his cold, empty apartment disagreed.

So did the empty bed.

# CHAPTER FOURTEEN

HEATHER WOKE THE next morning, ready to pack. She'd already called a real estate agent who would be there that afternoon to appraise her property. The land value probably remained the same as it had only been a few months since she'd purchased the place. But the new bathroom and kitchen had undoubtedly raised the value of the house. She would get back her investment and then some.

She kept her brain filled with useless thoughts like that because her heart couldn't take it if she thought about her real troubles. She'd been ready to give up her normal life for Axel and he'd acted as if what she'd suggested had been ridiculous.

Meaning, it had been ridiculous to love him. Ridiculous to fall in love with him.

It didn't matter. She'd gifted him—gifted *them*—with one final night and now she had to move on. She'd already been in contact with her former CO—commanding officer—who had contacts in the world of bodyguards. This time next week, she could be babysitting a rock star.

The idea almost made her laugh, but she still had that crazy pain around her breastbone. Her heart actually ached. She didn't kid herself into thinking she'd get rid of the sense of loss anytime soon. But she also refused to let herself dwell on how the loss of one very important person could reduce her to a mushy ball of sadness.

She heard the sounds of a helicopter long before she saw it land in the tall grass on the edge of her property. Confused, she stood on the quaint back porch with slim, whittled-down tree trunks for pillars and a bare wood floor.

Blades slowing, the helicopter settled to a stop and the side door opened. Axel jumped out.

Her heart shot to triple time, but she reminded herself that he had hurt her. Not intentionally. Truth be told, she'd known they were only having a fling. And going one step deeper into the truth, she also knew he was hurting as much as she did. Even if he believed he was doing the right thing.

But the same heart that was beating at three times its normal speed had loved him. It had seen his hurts and his pains. That was the part that had shrunk to a soft ball of heartache when she'd realized she'd fallen and he hadn't. He couldn't. He'd shoved down his emotions so much he had no way to access them. All he saw was the day before him and the possibility of being happy.

That's what he'd been doing with her. Escaping with her. Enjoying what they had. When he woke and found her gone, he'd probably taken a breath, felt the loss, then put his feet on the floor and told himself to get up, make the best of the day.

So what was he doing here two days later?

He raced across her untamed field of tall grass with a smattering of wildflowers turning their multicolored faces to the sun.

He stopped at the bottom step of her porch and looked up at her. "You left some things in my apartment."

"No, I didn't. I took everything I brought."

"I have an entire closet of clothes that says differently."

"Castle Admin bought those. They aren't mine. Plus, I don't want them. Don't need them."

"But they were bought for you."

"They were bought for the *charade*. I can assure you I won't need them for my next bodyguard job."

"You have a job?"

"I have irons in the fire."

"But no job?"

"Give me a break. It's been two days. I'll have a job before I go back to the States."

"So you're leaving Prosperita?"

"What did you think I was going to do?"

He shrugged. "This is such a neat cabin, I thought you might make it your home base."

"Nope. Selling it."

He paused a second. "Selling it?"

"Real estate agent is coming today."

He looked tired and she could see his whole life stretching out before him as long and lonely. Still, she couldn't help him. It wasn't her job to rescue him. These were his choices.

"I miss you."

Well, damn, if that didn't hit her right in the heart. He missed her, not because he needed her. He'd shown her he was too strong to need anyone. But he did like her. If he missed her, it was because they were good together. Fun. And she'd missed him too.

She straightened her shoulders. She wasn't going to say it back. She had some pride. Lots of pride. Pride she hadn't even tapped into yet.

"This would be so much easier if I had a glass slipper to put on your foot."

Her face scrunched. "What?"

He took a breath. "I made a mistake. No." He shook his head. "I didn't make a mistake. I needed some time to think things through and I realized that I do love you."

Her heart stopped. *He loved her.* He'd said what she'd been longing to hear, but sometimes love did not conquer all. They had two different upbringings. They had two different ways of looking at life. They might fit, but there were glitches.

That's why he'd let her go and why she'd understood her heartbreak and was moving on. She had a real estate agent coming. Her commanding officer was circulating her name and résumé to his contacts.

Her decisions had been made.

"I didn't just come to ask you to be my vice president for the charitable foundation. Though I need you to fill that role. You're the one who came up with the idea. I think we should see it through together. Be a team."

She told her fluttering heart to stop. It sounded wonderful. It sounded amazing—but once again she'd be working for him. They might play, they might make love and take care of each other—but there'd never be a commitment, especially not a public commitment.

"But I really came here to ask you to be my wife." He reached into the back pocket of his jeans and pulled out a small jeweler's box. Levering himself on one knee two steps below her, he said, "Will you marry me?"

A beautiful ring winked at her. She wasn't the kind of woman who stopped at the window of jewelry stores and sighed over beautiful diamonds, so she had no idea what size it was. But it was big. More than that, it was sparkly. Every single facet seemed to catch the light and shimmer with beauty.

Her heart stuttered. Her soul begged her to simply say yes and jump into his arms and the warmth she knew waited there.

Her pragmatic side told her heart to settle down.

They'd spent weeks together. The last night she'd longed for him to tell her he loved her. There hadn't needed to be a ring. His words would have sealed the commitment for her.

But he hadn't said them the last night they were together. He might have said them when he'd first arrived at her cabin, but they had both been through two difficult days when emotion could overrule facts. If she believed him and left with him, a few days from now, sated and happy, reality could set in. And he could change his mind about marriage. Rearrange things so that they lived together in private, and she was his bodyguard, or vice president and good friend in public.

"I thought your life was too difficult to drag a partner into?"

He laughed. "If anyone can handle it, it's you. And I miss you. I realized what you'd been seeing after only a few weeks. We belong together."

How was a woman not supposed to jump on that? His words were beautiful, almost poetic. But she'd been burned before.

"The night I left you made it clear you didn't believe that."

"The night you left I was an idiot. I'd spent my life denying I had feelings. It took me a few days to realize I do have feelings. For you. I realized all the other women I dated were lovely, but you were different. Special. Maybe even made for me. And I sort of like the idea."

She stared at him.

"I had feelings with you from day one and couldn't stomp them down, couldn't pretend they didn't exist, couldn't explain them away. When I realized yesterday that was because I wanted to feel all that, it was life changing."

A laugh began to bubble up. "Life changing, huh?"

He got off his knee and climbed the first step toward her. "Yes."

The gleam came to his eyes, the one she loved, the one that told her there was something about her he couldn't resist.

"You were sort of life changing for me too."

He climbed another step. "Certainly took you long enough to admit it."

"I had a bad marriage."

He climbed the last step and she put her arms around his shoulders. "I've lived an unusual life."

"All those things make you perfect for me."

He kissed her so long she was breathless from it. When he stepped away, he whispered, "I love you. I may have loved you from our first date, when you invited the gossip columnist to have drinks with us. I knew you were different but it was a good different."

She laughed, but her eyes filled with tears. She'd never met anyone who liked her just as she was…quirks and all. And she'd never met anyone she seemed to make as happy as he made her.

"I love you too."

He produced the ring again. "Are we making this official?"

Her tears spilled over. "Yes."

"We've got so many announcements to make and Rowan's definitely going to want an engagement ball." He slid the ring on her finger, then glanced around. "Can we keep the cabin?"

She laughed through her tears. "I was just going to ask you the same thing."

"Good, because I hear there's a new kitchen in here and someone promised to teach me how to cook."

She grabbed his shirt collar and yanked him to her so she could kiss him again. She heard the sound of the helicopter leaving and wasn't sure if his pilot had gotten tired of waiting for him or if he'd told him that if things looked like they were going well he should take off and give them some alone time—

Either way, she kissed him until the sound went away, then she caught his hand and led him into the kitchen, where she showed him how to make an omelet, which they shared before she showed him the brand-new primary suite with the fancy bathroom.

# EPILOGUE

THEY WED IN the spring because Heather liked the association to new things, new life. She wore a white silk dress that caught the sunlight and made it appear that she was glowing.

She was, of course. Her entire family and half of her small town had shown up for the wedding. Axel knew most of them were there purely out of curiosity, but it had been important to him that she knew her life—her family, her friends, her world—was as important as his.

Because it was. After all the women he'd dated, all the beautiful women who walked into his life, she was the one who was a true partner. Sexy, smart, able to hold her own in any situation, she was the woman he'd been waiting for.

The sentiment filled him with awe. When the minister told him he could kiss the bride, he kissed her hand out of overwhelming love and anticipation of their life together, then pulled in her for the long, lingering kiss that sealed their union.

When they broke the kiss, she slid her hand

around his elbow, her maid of honor handed her bouquet to her and they walked down the aisle under the canopy of white roses.

At the reception in the main ballroom of the castle, they danced their first dance to her favorite song. Then their parents joined them on the floor, then the bridal party.

His happiness tempered for the moment, Axel glanced at his brother. "He seems to be doing okay."

Heather shook her head. "It was horrid of Lilibet to break up with him so close to the wedding."

"Liam said she had her reasons and that we should let it alone."

Heather growled. "You know that—first and foremost—I'm in favor of letting people live their own lives, but this is just so confusing."

He twirled her around once.

"They were so perfect." She sighed. "Something had to have happened."

Axel winced. "Something did happen."

She stopped dancing. "You know why she broke up with him?"

He caught her up and twirled her around again, so no one would notice she was more interested in their conversation than enjoying their wedding. "I'll tell you, but you can't react."

"I know how to behave."

He couldn't help it. He kissed her. "Yes. You do."

"So? What was her reason for breaking up with him?"

"She did it *for* him."

Heather frowned. "That makes no sense."

"Actually, it makes perfect sense." Axel drew a quick breath. "She can't have children."

Heather froze. He hustled her back into step before anyone saw.

"Oh, my God."

"I know you believe this antiquated, but Liam's greatest duty to his country is to produce an heir. He was ready to give up the throne for her. She wouldn't let him."

Heather's eyes filled with tears. "That's so awful."

"Yeah. That's why we have to keep an eye on him for a while, make sure he doesn't do anything foolish."

"I will."

He twirled her again before the music stopped. "I know you will. But right now, we are in the middle of the biggest day of our lives. Liam would shoot us if we don't enjoy it."

She pulled in a breath. "Yeah." Her eyes narrowed. "So why'd you tell me? Why not save it?"

He laughed. "Oh, you're so fickle. This time last year you got angry with me for not sharing details of the manhunt around my shooting. Now you want me to keep secrets?"

She shook her head. "No."

He put her out of her misery. "He just told me

when we were getting pictures taken. I think he held it in as long as he could. So, basically, I told you the first real chance I got."

She smiled. "Oh."

"No more secrets."

Her eyes filled with love. "No more secrets."

"No more charades."

Her smile grew. "No more charades. Though the first one did sort of end up pretty good for us."

He kissed her again. "Sure did."

And she laughed. The sound so light and so happy, his heart expanded. The life he believed would be mundane or pointless had found real meaning and purpose. Together they were going to change the world.

\* \* \* \* \*

*Look out for the next story in the*
*Scandal at the Palace trilogy*
*Coming soon!*

*And, if you enjoyed this story,*
*check out these other great reads*
*from Susan Meier*

One-Night Baby to Christmas Proposal
His Majesty's Forbidden Fling
The Single Dad's Italian Invitation

*All available now!*